out of sight

A FORBIDDEN, AGE GAP, FORCED PROXIMITY ROMANCE

CLEO WHITE

Edited by Lauren, The Eclectic Editor

Cover Design by Books and Moods

❈ Created with Vellum

FROM:	E.BRADLEY@COLUMBIAMED.COM
TO:	C.HOLMESBRADLEY@NYCMED.COM, JBRADLEY@NYCMED.COM, R.HALE@COLUMBIAMED.COM, J.HALE@CDC.GOV, KENNEDY@LUCASREALTY.COM, NOLAN@LUCAS REALTY.COM, TOM@LUCASREALTY.COM, I.BRADLEY@UCHICAGO.EDU

SUBJECT: DAY 1: WELCOME TO BORA BORA!

Hello Lucas/Bradley/Hale Family Members!

Reuben and I want to officially welcome everyone to our wedding week! Flight delays and other scheduling issues beyond our control have arisen, so please make sure to check your emails regularly for reminders on the itinerary and notices of any changes.

Please remember to pack your bug spray and sunscreen on all outings, though the resort gift shop does sell both if need be.

Dinner begins at 6:45 PM tonight (local time) in the resort's "Sunspot Restaurant," which offers a full range of vegan, vegetarian, gluten-free menu options, so there should be something for everyone!

Thank you again to everyone for making the journey.

Evie & Reuben

one

"GOING ON VACATION?"

I blink, tearing my eyes from my computer screen to find the old woman in the seat beside mine gazing at me expectantly.

"Um. No. I'm going to my sister's wedding." I shut my laptop, giving her the same pained, obligatory smile I usually reserve for the girl in my chem class who licks her fingers before turning the pages of our *shared* lab packet. Not that it matters. I could probably bare my teeth and growl at this woman, and it wouldn't put her off. We've been on this plane for three hours, and she's tried to make conversation with me at least six times, apparently mistaking my utter lack of interest for shyness.

Isn't there a rule in the airplane safety pamphlet about leaving the stranger next to you alone, or is that just common courtesy?

The woman—whom I mentally dubbed "Old Bat" before the plane had even taken off—lights up, clasping her hands to her chest like I told her Evie cured an incurable disease. Joke's on her, though. Evie isn't scheduled to cure

1

pediatric pleuropulmonary blastoma for another four years. Considering my sister still hasn't deviated from the life plan she finalized at age fourteen, I'd hold her to that. "How *exciting*! A destination wedding? Are you the Maid of Honor?"

Holy hell. I feel like I'm staring into an intellectual black hole.

"Yup." I'm not, nor did I expect to be, but Old Bat doesn't need to know that. My sister is six years older than I am. By the time I was old enough to speak in full sentences, she was off to boarding school. We never had those formative years of bickering and bonding, and now the only thing we have in common is our eye color and the undying urge to please our parents. This trip, a full week in Bora Bora for her wedding, will be the most time I've spent with any of my family members in years.

I've met my future brother-in-law, Reuben, only once, and that was at my grandmother's Passover seder last year. We didn't speak much but, from what I could tell, he seemed like exactly the kind of guy Evie would always end up with—intelligent and easygoing enough to balance out her type-A neurosis. They met on the very first day of medical school, but didn't start dating until they were placed into the same pediatric oncology residency, falling in love over kids with cancer and after-work espresso martinis.

Old Bat beams. "Oh, I was the maid of honor for my sister. She got married in Florida the year... *oh*. When was it? Well, anyway, they divorced only a few years later because—"

Alright, I'm out.

My noise-canceling headphones died just as I was getting

on the plane, but Old Bat doesn't know that. Not bothering to make up an excuse, I pull them out of my bag and snap them on while she's halfway through the word "potpourri." I can see her offended pout in the corner of my eye, but I stare determinedly down at my phone, aimlessly scrolling until she's safely turned away to talk to the poor flight attendant. Reflexively, I reopen my laptop, hitting refresh on my email for the third time in the last fifteen minutes.

Why hasn't it come yet?

Everything I've worked for, the parties I didn't go to, and the countless late nights in the library, have all come down to one email.

Going to Weston Medical School is what the Bradley family *does*. My great-grandfather started the tradition before going on to become one of the founding fathers of cardiothoracic surgery. My grandfather followed in his footsteps, developing a procedure that has saved thousands of lives. Then my father, who met and later married my equally brilliant mother there, undoubtedly hoping to create an elite, hybrid generation of Doctor Bradleys to conquer the world one medical innovation at a time.

It half worked.

I know I'm not an idiot, but as I head into the final semester of my undergraduate education, it seems pretty ridiculous to pretend I'm a match for my sister. Evie graduated a year early with honors, perfect test scores, a letter of recommendation from the dean, and a handful of prestigious internships under her belt. All with a flawless manicure, a pack of loyal girlfriends, and an apartment that could have been on the cover of *Organized Living*.

I am graduating a year late because of that semester off. I've been advised—ordered—never to mention a non-existent social life and an academic record that's good but not exceptional.

Also, her boobs are, like, twice the size of mine. Talk about some bullshit.

Something in my chest knots painfully, and I force myself to take a long, slow breath. It's going to be fine. I'm being ridiculous. I might not be as utterly, incomprehensibly perfect as Evie, but that doesn't mean I won't get in. I've worked hard, I have recommendations from my professors, and I've been volunteering for over two years. If all that doesn't seal the deal, I'm not too proud to rely on the three generations of Weston alumni who share my last name for some of those sweet nepotism points.

"Good afternoon, passengers. The captain has turned on the fasten seatbelt sign—"

The clouds clear away as the plane drops lower, and now I can see a beautiful island settled atop the crystal-clear ocean beyond the wing of the plane. My parents went all out, buying out half of a boutique Bora Bora resort for Evie and Reuben's wedding—the very same one that they were married at nearly thirty years ago.

The immediate families of the bride and groom will be arriving today, five full days early, and we'll be joined by the rest of the guests the night before the wedding. Evie wanted my parents to get to know Reuben's by doing what she does best: organizing. She emailed everyone a five-page, color-coded schedule, which includes helpful reminders to regularly re-apply sunscreen and hydrate. Our parents and I will be subjected to five full days of forced bonding activities and wedding organizing with these strangers before my sister deems us sufficiently integrated and we're permitted to return to our separate corners of the country.

Beneath me, the plane jerks, and I grip my armrests so hard that my knuckles turn white, prompting an alarmed look from Old Bat.

I know it's not normal to feel this way before seeing your family, and that there's probably a therapist out there who will someday make a lot of money off me, but normally I can handle it. I was counting on having a med-school acceptance to lessen their general disappointment in me, though, and my Weston-free inbox has notched my anxiety up to a near-critical level.

They're going to ask about it, *of course*, they're going to ask about it, and I feel sick just thinking about the pursed lips and quiet sighs I'll get when I tell them, *"No, I haven't heard yet."* They haven't said it out loud, but I can't quite manage to dismiss the gnawing suspicion that I've already been sort of... written off.

Having high-powered surgeons as parents tends to translate into a certain level of emotional neglect. I'm used to that, but it's been impossible not to form parallels between those months before Evie applied to medical school and when I did. They were so excited for her. My mother was constantly calling to discuss application essay questions and which apartment buildings they ought to look at, while my father conveniently invited an old friend who works in the admissions office to dinner.

There'd been none of that for me. Is it because they think I don't have a chance of getting in, or—

No. I shove the thought aside.

They've been busy, that's all. Evie's wedding is coming up, my mother is up for that big award, and my father's practice partner retired earlier than planned, so his case-load has been crazy. Those are all perfectly valid reasons for them not calling me every hour to talk about Weston. I'm

5

being selfish. This is Evie's wedding week and, no matter how shitty our parents make me feel, I refuse to make it even a little bit about me.

I keep my eyes on the runway as the plane makes its final descent, palm trees and crystalline waters flashing by until we land with a jerk, bumping and skidding toward a small airport with only half a dozen planes outside.

The moment the flight attendants open the doors, a wall of humidity and the scent of the nearby ocean hit me like a wall. Old Bat takes her time gathering up her free copy of *Air Times Magazine*, three unopened bags of peanuts, and a fuzzy purple neck pillow before finally rising and allowing me to escape the suddenly unbearable, claustrophobic plane onto the hot tarmac.

It's nearly noon, and the sun is high. So, by the time I get my bags from the luggage claim and drag them out to the line of hotel shuttles and taxis, my t-shirt is clinging to my back, and I'm panting. A quick glance at myself in my phone's camera is enough to confirm I look exactly as shitty as I knew I would after spending fifteen hours getting on and off planes, sitting next to overly chatty old ladies, and eating fistfuls of flavorless snacks in between bouts of uncomfortable sleep.

In other words, *really* shitty.

As far as I know, no one in our family or Reuben's will be arriving until later this afternoon. With any luck, I should be able to escape to my hotel room unnoticed and clean up before dinner tonight—the first event on Evie's schedule.

I want to collapse in relief when I finally find a white shuttle van adorned with the logo of the Regency Sun Resort & Spa, the driver leaning against it with a cigarette between his fingers. He throws it away as I approach, giving my body an appreciative look as he welcomes me to Bora Bora in heavily accented English. "You are not the bride, no?" he asks as I climb up into the van.

He's objectively attractive, maybe a year or two older than me with floppy brown hair and golden-brown skin; the perfect vacation fling, if you're into that sort of thing. I'm positive I'm not the only pretty foreigner he's made eyes at, nor will I be the last. I almost wish I could. Having someone to take my mind off Weston and the family stress would be great, but, unfortunately, I've learned the hard way that rationalizing someone's attractiveness isn't actually going to make me attracted to them.

"No, I'm not the bride," I assure him quietly, settling back in my seat and brushing the sticky strands of hair out of my face. The van is thankfully air-conditioned, but the flirty driver makes no move to shut the door.

"We have another guest arriving," he tells me over his shoulder just as another exhausted-looking traveler approaches, dragging a suitcase with a garment bag slung over his arm and dressed in wrinkled clothes.

I still, my chest suddenly tight.

The newcomer must be in his mid-forties, but he's in better shape than the driver, who is half his age. Broad-shouldered and tall, he towers over the travelers walking past him on the sidewalk, checking the logo on the van from behind thick-framed black glasses. He looks like a silver-haired Clark Kent, and I realize with a jolt I've been pressing my thighs together as heat pools low in my belly.

Um. What?

"Regency Sun?" confirms the driver, glancing over his shoulder at me with a sly little smile, like we're in on a secret.

"That's right," the newcomer says, his voice low and weary. "How far are we from the resort?"

"Oh, about fifteen minutes, very easy drive," the driver informs him, taking the man's luggage around to the back.

I watch, my lungs burning with a breath I can't quite manage to exhale, as the stranger casts a long, lasting look over his shoulder like he's looking for someone. Shaking his head slightly, he turns and moves to the van's open door, making to step up. When our eyes meet, however, he stops dead, staring at me.

There might be some staring back. Because, holy shit, he's hot. Really hot. Even sticky with sweat and clearly just as ruffled from sitting on an airplane as I am. My cheeks warm. Oh god, I look so bad right now. But he's still looking at me; not my body, but straight into my eyes.

A metallic thud makes both of us jump, and the stranger's eyes finally move from mine to the van floor, where his phone has fallen from his hand and is lying face down on the metal frame around the door. Cursing quietly, he picks it up, wincing at the spiderweb of cracks running through the screen.

Oops.

"Sir?" The driver is back, and the newcomer shoves the device in his pocket before stepping up inside. This van has four rows of seats, but he takes the one across the aisle from me.

It feels like my whole body is suddenly attached to a live wire. My entire consciousness is focused on the stranger sitting just a few feet away from me, and my heart is suddenly hammering frantically against my ribcage. This has *never* happened to me. Ever. I have several ex-boyfriends who could attest to my complete disinterest in them.

I always rolled my eyes at the girls in school who became gooey, fluttery messes when the right boy smiled their way, but I'm feeling pretty gooey and fluttery right now.

"Where are you coming from?"

I look around so quickly that a muscle in my neck spasms painfully. "Oh!" I rub it, wincing. His voice is *great*, low, and just a little gravely. "Sorry. I've clearly been sitting on a plane for too long. Um, I'm here from Chicago, but I flew through Tahiti. You?"

He grins sheepishly, like I've caught him in the act. "Washington D.C. But I, ah, was on the same connecting flight. I noticed you."

Oh. Okay, wow. I hope he didn't hear me stonewall Old Bat when she asked me the same question he just did.

The front door slams as the driver climbs in, turning to give me a crooked smile that is obviously designed to be charming. "We'll be at the resort in no time," he tells me smoothly, completely ignoring his other passenger. "Please let me know if you need anything to improve your stay, Miss..." He trails off, waiting for me to give my name.

I grimace, but before I can make something up, my stranger does. "Mrs," he informs the driver nonchalantly, so casually he might have been reporting the weather conditions. Without hesitation, he reaches across the aisle to weave his fingers through my hand where it's resting in my lap. "We're here for our anniversary."

The driver's lips pinch like he doesn't quite believe him, but thankfully turns back around and directs his attention to the road, fiddling with the radio as we pull into airport traffic.

My stranger doesn't release my hand, though. "Should I hold your hand a while longer, just to be safe?" he asks under his breath, the corner of his lips lifting in a mischievous smile. There's something about him that screams *professional*, like he spends his days in a suit and knows how to create one hell of a spreadsheet, but when he smiles....

Butterflies. Actual butterflies erupt inside me. Holy hell, I'm twenty-three years old. It's a little late for a first crush.

"I—Yes. Yes, please." I can't believe this is happening. It's like I've stumbled out of a depressing black-and-white indie movie into a rom-com meet cute. Or I would, if it weren't for the fact he's at least twenty years older than me, and I'm pretty much the definition of emotionally unavailable. I can flirt with him, though, can't I? "So, our anniversary, huh? How many years? In case he asks, of course."

"*Of course*," my stranger agrees solemnly, his eyes sparkling behind his glasses. "Two years, I think."

I hum thoughtfully, loving the feeling of his skin against mine and how his thumb drags slowly over the side of my hand, almost unconsciously. "Why two?"

His low chuckle goes right through me, spreading warmth that has nothing to do with the tropical climate. "We arrived at the shuttle separately, didn't we? It would take at least two years for me to be able to let you out of my sight. Do you know what? No. Three. Definitely three."

Cue exponential increase of gooey and fluttery feelings.

Is this actually happening? This isn't me. I'm awkward, prickly, and generally unsociable. My own family doesn't like spending time with me, and I've been operating under the assumption that if the people genetically obligated to like me don't, why would anyone else? I don't ever go out of my way to talk to people, but there's something in how this guy looks at me that makes all those usual worries disappear.

"Don't you think you should learn my name before signing up for that kind of commitment?"

His answering bark of laughter makes my heart feel full. "No." He shakes his head, still grinning. "Tell me anyway. It might be useful."

"Isobel."

His smile grows bigger. "Judah."

From the front seat, the driver has his eyes on me in the rearview mirror as he calls back, "How long have you been married?"

He looks back at the road when Judah and I respond in unison, "Three years!"

two

JUDAH

THE REGENCY SUN RESORT & Spa is a sprawling compound of thatched-roof, over-water bungalows clustered in small groups around the resort's many amenities. It's the kind of place that belongs on the cover of a travel magazine or on a bus bench advertisement, but not somewhere I ever thought I'd see for myself.

Unless you count the bus trip my tenth-grade band class made to Florida, I've never taken a vacation. It's an embarrassing admission for a man my age, and god knows I won't tell a soul. Even admitting it to myself is cringeworthy.

I was thrust into adulthood as a young, already divorced father, trying to force my way through medical school and residency with nothing but sheer grit and determination. Any spare time I had went to my son, and any money I had went to my ex-wife. Then my life became about growing my practice, trying to parent a disinterested teenager, and eventually navigating the tangled political circles in D.C.

All the while, I was never quite able to shake the work ethic born from being a teenage father who wanted out of his shitty hometown.

I *did* get out. I've been out a long time, but haven't acted like it. I've kept my head down and kept working, as if stopping meant it all would come crumbling down and I'd be back to square one. It's gut-wrenching to suddenly have the invitation to your only son's wedding in your hands and realize you'll never have that. He's an adult now, will probably have his own kids soon, and *damn me*—I'm fucking jealous.

It's not rational. I'm an OB/GYN. How many babies have I delivered at this point in my career? How many ecstatic new parents have I congratulated? How is it possible that in all that time, I never thought about having more children myself? How did I never wonder what it would feel like to be the excited, terrified man standing beside my patient in the delivery room?

The whole universe was throwing up ten-foot-tall *"Reevaluate Your Life Choices"* signs, and I was too locked in highway hypnosis to notice them. I have no one to blame but myself, but the gnawing, disquieting feeling of regret never let up. Or it *didn't* until I finished digging around in my carry-on bag for my phone charger before my last connecting flight took off and straightened up just in time to see a young woman with dark-blonde hair slide into the seat two rows up from mine.

I barely had a glimpse of her, and still, I felt... fucking obsessed. I looked up whenever there was movement in the aisles, hoping for another sighting of her, but didn't get one apart from the back of her head when the plane disembarked. I thought about her at the customs line, and while scrolling through the emails on my phone to check the name of the resort. I even cast a few hopeful looks over the people waiting along the line of taxis and hotel shuttles.

I didn't plan on bothering her—I know a lost cause when I see one—but I still couldn't resist one last look over my shoulder when I got to the shuttle.

It's a miracle I didn't have a heart attack when I finally stepped into the van and met the warm, brown eyes of the woman from the plane. She was even more beautiful up close, a fucking goddess in yoga pants and a wrinkled t-shirt, and it was like every cell in my body ignited in unison at the sight of her. The extraordinary thing, though, the thing I never expected, was that she was looking right back at me.

Every time I see the cracks spreading over the screen of my phone, something heady and pleasurable curls up my spine as I remember how they got there.

Isobel.

When we got to the hotel, we walked side by side into the lobby, my hand pressed to the small of her back to make sure that little shit of a driver didn't try anything, and only separated at the reception desk. They'd mixed up my reservation and Reuben's, so I had to stand there watching helplessly while the hotel porter whisked Isobel's bags onto a trolly, and she gave me a shy little smile over her shoulder as they left.

We're staying at the same resort. I knew I would likely bump into her again, but the moment she walked out the door, I knew that *probably* wasn't good enough. I have enough regrets. I refuse to go back to D.C. with one more "*what if?*". The poor woman at reception was only halfway through running through the various amenities and activities available for guests when I pushed off the desk, sprinting through the lobby and outside into the bright sun.

I spotted her immediately, trailing after the porter and looking off toward the beach.

"Isobel!" She turned, eyes widening in surprise as I jogged toward her, heart in my throat.

When I stopped in front of her, though, I was suddenly lost. "I, uh—" I'm not sure why it occurred to me then, more than any of the other moments leading up to it, but it hit me that I'm way too old for this woman. I had no business asking for her number. What the hell was I thinking, chasing her down? I'm probably bothering her...

But apparently, I wasn't. Isobel's eyes crinkled, and she reached into her pocket, pulling out her phone. "Maybe you should give me your number. I'll text you so you have mine. Since we're married and all, I might need to get in touch with you for tax season."

It was just a goddamn joke, but fuck me if I didn't like those words on her lips. Maybe it's yet another sign that I'm getting old, but I don't remember ever feeling this burning, possessive attraction to a woman, never mind one I barely know. All it took was one look at her, and my whole soul *woke up*.

She *did* text me, before I'd even made it ten steps back to the lobby, making my chest swell with smug, male pride when I glanced back and caught her watching me walk away.

"I'll call you," I called, and she turned back toward the bungalows, casting me one last look over her shoulder with her bottom lip caught between her teeth.

Our entire time together couldn't have been longer than twenty minutes, and yet I haven't stopped thinking about her in the four hours since I got here, turning over every second of our interaction in my mind. Every time I've half-heartedly managed to rationalize away the whole thing as sexual frustration or a midlife crisis or *something*, catching sight of those fine cracks over my phone screen is all it takes to be back at square one.

She's *young*, almost certainly younger than my own son, and I'm a little appalled at *how little I give a damn*. I'm not the sort of man who chases pretty young women in a feeble attempt to escape my own mortality. On the rare occasion I break out of my routine enough to go on a few dates, the women I see are self-assured, successful, and age appropriate. The sex is satisfying, but rarely repeated.

They aren't sweet little twenty-somethings with wide eyes and mischievous smiles that make me want tò hand-cuff her to my bed and throw away the key. Isobel is very much the exception, not the rule, but an exception I intend to pursue.

That is, if I can manage to find a few spare hours in the schedule my future daughter-in-law emailed me.

I've only met Reuben's fiancée a handful of times, but I did my obstetrics fellowship at the same hospital where both of her parents work. While I wouldn't call her parents and I friends, we run in the same circles. Evie seems a lot like her mother: intelligent and dignified, if a bit tightly wound.

I'm just about to leave for the first event of the week—dinner with the Bradley's, my ex-wife, her husband, and their son—when there's a knock on my bungalow's door.

"Hey, old man," Reuben greets me, grinning from behind aviator sunglasses when I open it.

I smile too, hugging him tightly. We've gotten closer the last few years since he graduated from medical school. He now understands a little more of my struggle when he was young, and any lingering resentment for missed T-ball games or school plays has long since been put to rest. He was always a good kid, but he's grown into a great man, and I consider myself lucky. Incredibly lucky.

"When did you get in?" I ask, stepping back to allow him into the spacious living room.

"Last night. Evie wanted a chance to scope everything out. She hasn't been here since she was a kid, and it's changed a lot." He leans against the kitchen island, looking around appraisingly. "Quite a place, right?"

It really is. My bungalow includes a great room, spacious bathroom, and bedroom, but the most breathtaking part of the place is the back deck which sprawls out over the crystal-clear ocean. When I bought a pair of swim trunks in D.C., I wasn't particularly looking forward to using them, but maybe with the right company...

"Dad?" I blink, looking back at Reuben, who stares at me questioningly.

"Sorry." I shake my head, trying to clear away thoughts of what Isobel might look like in a bikini. "Jet lag."

Reuben nods sympathetically. "Me too. Well, on the bright side, I just heard from Mom. She and Tom were delayed and missed their connecting flight, so we won't see them until tomorrow afternoon. It'll just be us and the Bradleys for dinner."

"Sounds good." I grab my phone from the table, running my thumb over the hairline cracks on the screen as I slip it into my pocket. Truthfully, I'm glad for a few hours to spend with Reuben and Evie before my ex-wife demands most of their attention. Kennedy has always been the life of the party, a great partner to a man like her husband, Tom, who owns a luxury real estate brokerage. They're far better suited to each other than Kennedy and I could ever have been, and our marriage was so short-lived it feels like another life now. Her second son, Reuben's half-brother, Nolan, is a great kid too.

Reuben and I chat about his residency and the upcoming wedding as we stroll over the boardwalk, which connects the bungalows to the main resort area. I'm determined to be present for this and give my future in-laws my full attention, but I can't help scanning the pool area, tennis courts, and lobby, hoping in vain for a glimpse of Isobel.

We find Evie waiting on the patio of the resort's seafood restaurant, wearing a white silk dress and standing with her parents.

"Judah!" John chuckles as we approach, holding out a hand to shake mine enthusiastically. "Isn't life funny? The last time we saw you was at that conference in Aspen. When was that, Caroline?" He looks to his wife, who smiles as she leans forward to kiss my cheek.

"Four years ago. Well before the kids started dating." She beams, moving over to embrace Reuben. "When is your mother getting in, Reu?"

"Not until late," he tells her obligingly, wrapping an arm around Evie's waist. "They'll join us for sailing tomorrow, though."

"You know how to sail, now?" I chuckle, raising my eyebrows at my son. "When you were eight, you begged me to *forget* to sign your permission form for canoeing with your boy scout troop."

Everyone laughs, and Reuben rolls his eyes, huffing. "Save the embarrassing jokes for after the wedding when she's stuck with me."

"Sailing is a Bradley family pastime." John boasts, nodding toward the stunning strip of beach beyond the restaurant patio. "Evie was always a natural."

"Let's sit," I suggest, gesturing to the neatly set table behind our group. "I need a drink after that flight. Dinner is my treat, everyone."

Reuben shakes his head. "We're waiting for Evie's sister."

"Sister?" I've known John and Caroline for years, and I'm positive they've never mentioned a second daughter. They brag about Evie's accomplishments constantly, to the point of it being a little obnoxious. Whatever internal speculation I have about the unknown Bradley sister dies immediately, however, when my future daughter-in-law looks past my right shoulder and brightens.

"Isobel!"

No. No way. It couldn't be her—

"Hey, everyone."

Even before I turn, I know who I'll see standing behind me. Her voice is softer, less confident than on the shuttle, but it raises the same prickle of awareness up my spine. I'm prepared, but I still feel an agonizing stab of disappointment when I turn and see Isobel moving toward me. She's dressed in a dark-blue dress that whispers over her curves like the ocean visible in the distance, and her hair is loose around her slim shoulders. She looks older, more mature, and yet the sparkle of life behind her beautiful face is dulled now.

She's the most beautiful woman I've ever seen.

Her steps falter when her eyes meet mine, a flicker of shock registering across her face before it returns to smooth impassivity so quickly I might have imagined it.

"Hello, darling. So glad you made it." Caroline breezes by me to kiss Isobel's cheek with the same perfunctory familiarity she just showed me.

"Hi, Mom. Dad." Her eyes move to John, who moves

forward to give her a brief, one-armed hug. "How, uh"—Her eyes flick to me, then back to her sister, a dull flush rising over her cheeks—"how was everyone's flight?"

"Oh, easy," Evie says as she takes her turn hugging her sister. Even side by side, I still can't see much of a resemblance between the two. Their eyes are the same shape and color, but Evie has their mother's tall, curvy physique and olive-skinned complexion, whereas Isobel is willowy and pale. And younger. Isobel is younger.

Christ. She's my future daughter-in-law's *little sister*, and I've been fantasizing all day about how she'd look on her knees, those beautiful lips wrapped around my cock while I fuck her mouth.

"Isobel, this is my father, Doctor Judah Hale," Reuben tells her, and I feel almost dizzy when Isobel looks back at me with a polite, guarded smile still in place.

"We've met," I reply before I can think better of it, and it's like a punch to the gut when I see Isobel's wince. Is she embarrassed she flirted with me or embarrassed to be found out by her family? The latter. *I hope*. "Briefly. On the airport shuttle. I think we were on the same connecting flight."

Evie brightens. "Oh, what a coincidence! Have you heard from Weston yet, Isobel?" She turns to look at me. "Isobel is going to be at Weston Med in the fall."

"Not yet," Isobel replies quietly, looking like she would rather be anywhere but here.

I'm not sure why the fact she's trying to be a physician is so surprising to me, but I'm struggling to reconcile that the woman who flirted with me on the shuttle was born into this family. Even the way she holds herself is so different than Caroline, Evie, or John, and it couldn't be clearer from their less than warm welcome that they aren't close. I want to ask her why she's applying and what's drawing her to medicine, but it's none of my business.

She's off limits now. I need to back off and do my best to put this behind me.

Pining after a woman half my age was dubious enough, but Evie's sister? Unthinkable.

three

IF I NEEDED any more evidence that there is something seriously wrong with me, this shitshow is pretty convincing.

I've gotten *close* to having sex before, with several perfectly nice boyfriends who did their best to ensure I enjoyed myself. I've masturbated too—with my fingers, with the little pink vibrator I ordered online, watching porn, reading filthy books—and all I got was *nothing*. No sparks, no earth-shattering orgasm, no heavenly angels singing from above. Just me laying amidst tangled sheets, feeling more frustrated and pent up than when it began.

I haven't bothered with any of it in a long time.

How Judah made me feel just by holding my hand is unprecedented. By the time we got off the shuttle, I'd been reduced to a fluttery, hot mess, torn between jumping his bones in the nearest public restroom and running away as fast as I could.

I still had yet to decide by the time I was supposed to meet everyone for dinner and ended up being late because I spent an extra fifteen minutes getting ready *just in case* I ran into him. He dropped his phone so hard the screen broke at the sight of me as a gross, international air travel gremlin. What would he do if he saw me when I was actually trying?

There might have been some fantasies of being dragged back to his place and fucked on every flat surface instead of going to dinner with my family. Because that thing I've always had to do, talk myself into being attracted to someone... I don't have to do that with him. Not even a little.

Of course, the first time I feel a flicker of the heat that gets so much hype, it's directed toward the most inappropriate man possible.

I stand there, listening to them all make small talk about Reuben and Evie's hospital and the department head, whom they all apparently can't stand. I have nothing to contribute to this discussion, just like most of the conversations my family has in my presence.

Mom eventually suggests we sit and leads the way over to our table. She, Dad, and me are on one side, with Judah, Evie, and Reuben on the other. Unhelpfully, Judah takes the seat right across from me. I bury my face in the menu, trying to give myself a chance to calm the hell down.

Avoidance–1

Dignity–0

It's not a proud moment. For once, I'm grateful for Evie being in the spotlight. Never before have I wanted to fly under their radar as badly as I do now. Obviously, I'm not going to put the moves on my sister's future father-in-law, and while Judah thankfully glossed over the finer points of our meeting earlier, I know it's probably because he's embarrassed. I was an ego boost, and I'm so desperate for connection that at the first hint of feeling something other than benign tolerance for a man, I practically threw myself at him.

Biting my lip, I realize the sharp, hollow feeling in my chest is disappointment. *I liked him.* I hardly like anyone, but I liked Judah.

How do I feel nothing for people who want me and everything for people who don't?

"Isobel?"

Shit. I drop the menu, fighting to keep my expression impassive even when I immediately meet Judah's bright-blue eyes, and I'm filled with the same eruption of butterflies as I was at the airport. *Haven't those little assholes got the memo that this can't happen?*

"Yes?" I drag my eyes over to Evie, who was the one who spoke.

She looks at me strangely. "I asked if you were volunteering for your applications."

I nod, grateful for the neutral topic. "Oh. Yes, I am. I really like it, so—"

"Judah," Mom interrupts, and my mouth snaps shut. "Will you tell us about the work you're doing? I heard you're with the CDC now?"

My eyes fall back to my menu, still not taking in a word of it. I should be used to her dismissive attitude—this is hardly out of character for my mother—but I haven't seen her in almost six months, and it still stings that she would rather catch up with Judah than hear about my life.

He clears his throat, and when he answers her, he sounds distracted. "Um. Yes. Yes, I'm with the CDC in addition to maintaining my practice. But Isobel, you were saying something about your volunteer work?"

I'm so taken aback that I look sharply up at him without meaning to. Beside me, I can feel the annoyance radiating from Mom in waves. Doctor Holmes-Bradley doesn't take kindly to being told off by anyone, and Judah's redirect of the conversation back onto me after she moved it off is bound to piss her off.

"Yes, Isobel." She recovers smoothly, making a show of setting down her glass and turning to look at me. "I think it was a wonderful idea to volunteer at the hospital. Excellent for your resume too."

Dad nods in agreement, not looking up from his own menu. "What department do they have you helping in again, pumpkin? I remember you telling me all about it during one of our chats, but I can't quite remember the specifics."

One of our chats? The only time Dad calls me is to... never. He never calls me. I don't remember the last time my father and I had a conversation that didn't revolve around the weather, Evie's most recent accomplishment, or whatever meal was on the table in front of us. A bitter, defiant part of me wants to say it, wants to tell the whole table he has never once *chatted* with me about my life.

I don't even volunteer at the hospital.

"Radiology," I lie instead, feeling the weight of five sets of eyes on me as I busy myself with unfolding my napkin and draping it over my lap.

"That's right." Dad hums. "An interesting choice."

Interesting is his word for dumbass.

Judah clears his throat loudly, taking the wine menu from the center of the table. "What does everyone think about a bottle of something special? To toast the occasion."

The conversation thankfully moves away from me and back onto the wedding. When the bottle of vintage wine arrives, Judah takes it from the waiter and stands to pour out glasses for everyone, his fingertips brushing mine when he hands mine back to me. "What do you think?" he asks quietly. Though I'm still not looking at him, I can feel the weight of his eyes on me as I take my first sip.

I wish I could say I'm one of the rare college students with an appreciation for fine wine, but to me, this just tastes like someone soaked old grapes in rubbing alcohol. "It's nice." I set it back in front of me, shooting him a quick, tight smile.

"You don't like it?"

I swallow the lump in my throat. "It's okay."

But a big hand has already reached out and plucked my glass out from in front of me, and I watch as he pours my helping into his own glass, already signaling the waiter.

"Isobel," hisses Mom, and I feel heat crawling up my cheeks. "Judah is treating us to dinner, and that is a very expensive bottle of wine. It's incredibly rude to ask for something else."

My stomach drops. "I'm sorry." I look up at Judah, whose face has gone ridged. *Shit.* "Please don't get me anything else. It really was okay—"

"You didn't ask. I offered," he says crisply, just as the waiter arrives at his side. Pointing to a line on the menu, he tells the man, "Please bring her a glass of this."

He looks annoyed. *Really annoyed.*

Mom's shoulders are tense, and I know mine are too. Why can't I ever do the right things? Say the right things? I've been on this island for less than a day, and already I've flirted with Evie's future father-in-law, insulted him, and embarrassed myself. Perfect.

Sensing the shift in mood, Dad clears his throat. "So, what made you want to go the public service route, Judah? I understand your practice has been doing incredibly well."

Across the table from me, Judah turns his gaze to Dad. "There's quite a large discrepancy in perinatal healthcare for women of color in D.C. and nationwide, really. I'm only one man and I can only see so many patients, so I joined a task force the CDC has formed to address the imbalance."

Oh good, so he's also an expert in vaginas and a feminist saint.

Everyone at the table agrees, praising Judah for his efforts, but he still doesn't look pleased. When my drink arrives, I thank him quietly and take a long sip, hoping the alcohol will cut through the paralyzing anxiety that's only tightened since I learned who he really is. It's good, really good, and I don't know why that hurts so much. What he thinks of me shouldn't matter to me this much, but I ache for the return of the easygoing, friendly man who smiled at me on the shuttle.

It was so easy to be happy around him.

When he gets up to use the bathroom, I wait a minute and follow, lingering awkwardly in the hall outside them until Judah emerges. He stops short at the sight of me, his jaw tight.

I take a deep breath. "Listen, I'm really sorry about the wine thing. I didn't mean to come off as ungrateful or anything." I reach into my purse and pull out a twenty-dollar bill, pressing it into his hands. "And about... you know. *Earlier.* I swear I didn't know."

Judah is frozen, staring at me with the bill held loosely in his hands, clearly startled. "You think I'm angry you didn't like the wine? And about... earlier?"

I shrug, already edging back toward the dining room. "I should go. I just wanted to apologize. I didn't want this week to be awkward or anything."

I hurry off before he can formulate a response. Being alone with him for too long seems dangerous, especially out of sight in darkened hallways, away from our family members. I wish I could shut off my attraction toward him and think of him as a purely paternal figure, but it seems like a lost cause. Seeing him all cleaned up, wearing that button-up shirt that is just a little too tight across his shoulders...

What the hell does this guy do when he isn't delivering babies and crusading for equality in women's healthcare? Deadlift canned goods at the soup kitchen? Save puppies from trees? I bet right at this moment there's a line of really hot, forty-year-old divorcées waiting outside his professionally organized, sustainably powered townhouse, just waiting for their chance to rip his scrubs off.

The thought makes a sour taste fill my mouth, and I have to bite back a scowl as I slip back into the chair beside my mother while she watches through narrowed eyes.

"We need to discuss—" she begins, her voice lowered so Reuben, who's sitting further down the table and chatting with Evie and Dad, doesn't hear. But whatever she has to say to me falls away when Judah returns to the table, looking far more relaxed than he did when I left him, smiling at the both of us.

"Isobel." He reaches into his pocket and pulls out the bill I passed him outside the bathroom. "You were walking back ahead of me, and I saw you drop this."

JUDAH

THE SUN HAS SET COMPLETELY when dinner finally ends, and I make it back to my villa, feeling hollowed out.

We were only at that table for a little more than an hour, but any respect or goodwill I'd previously felt toward John and Caroline Bradley died long before the end of it. Their preferential treatment of Evie over Isobel wasn't just noticeable, it was blatant.

To her credit, Evie tried to pull her sister into the conversation a few times, but all it took was a condescending comment from Caroline or a dismissive laugh from John to send Isobel back into her shell. She spent the entire meal staring at her plate, taking the smallest possible sips of her wine as though worried if she finished it, I would buy her another, and picking at her house salad while the rest of the table ate lobster.

That beautiful, glowing woman I glimpsed earlier today was reduced to a ghost by her parents, and I had to bite my tongue so many times that there's a swollen ridge along it now.

It couldn't have been clearer that any interest John and Caroline showed in her life over dinner was purely for my benefit, and I have no idea how I'll sit back and watch this shit for the next week. How the hell does it not bother Reuben? Does he not notice them fawning over Evie while treating Isobel like some distant cousin they're obliged to entertain?

For fuck's sake, she thought I was upset with her for not enjoying a drink *she didn't choose.*

My chest tightens at the memory of her guarded expression when she met me outside the bathroom as I wander distractedly through the darkened bungalow to the back deck, undoing the buttons of my shirt. Outside, apart from the gentle lapping of waves, the ocean is dark and quiet. It's beautiful here, peaceful, but I couldn't feel more at odds with my surroundings.

I want her, and I can't.

Bracing my hands on the railing, I drop my head and take several long, steadying breaths.

Maybe I'm getting old, but I don't remember ever feeling this burning, possessive need for a woman, never mind one I barely know. I can't get involved with her. Any attraction I might feel, any hopes I might have had that all those dramatic love-at-first-sight stories weren't complete bullshit, became irrelevant the moment I learned who she is.

It was nothing—a passing flirtation. I'll allow myself to be disappointed, keep my distance from her, and after this wedding is over, I'll get past it. That's all I can do.

I'm about to turn back and go inside for the night when my eye is caught by light shining from the nearest bungalow as the back doors open and someone steps out onto the porch.

Isobel.

I know it's her even before my eyes have adjusted to the light. I can see it in the delicate slope of her shoulders and the way she walks, somehow already so familiar to me. When I can make out more than her silhouette, it feels like all the air has been sucked from my lungs.

There's nothing indecent or inappropriate about what she's wearing. We're at an ocean-side resort, and I passed a few dozen women in the pool area on my way back here who were dressed in less. The longer I stare, though, the harder it is to look away. Small, tight breasts, generous hips, and a perky ass only halfway covered by those fucking scraps of material masquerading as a bathing suit. She is the sexiest thing I've ever seen, and I've never gotten hard this quickly in my life.

This isn't a kind of attraction I've felt before; it's something else, something deep and primal.

It wouldn't be enough to fuck her. What I want from Isobel Bradley... *It isn't normal.*

Biting back a groan, I squeeze my throbbing erection through my shorts, fighting the urge to slip my hand inside and stroke myself as I watch her tie her hair back and dip her toe into the dark ocean.

What the hell is wrong with me? I don't do shit like this. I'm a physician. I've made a career out of advocating for women's health, yet here I am, standing in the dark while holding my cock like a fucking voyeur as she toes the edge of the deck, gazing out over the moonlit ocean. I've never seen anything more beautiful, though. No woman has ever drawn me in like this before. It's *instinctual.* I'm a snake waiting in long grass for a chance to strike the little mouse, and turning away isn't an option.

I don't release the breath I'm holding until she dives

beneath the waves, escaping back into the bungalow before I can do something really stupid like get in the water with her. I don't feel better now that she's out of sight. I feel worse. I'm gripped with that same gnawing, fierce frustration you get when you've forgotten something important, except I know exactly what I need to make the feeling go away... I just can't have it.

Slamming the bathroom door behind me, I turn on the shower water as cold as it will go and strip off the rest of my clothes. The icy spray takes my breath away and burns my skin, but does nothing to relieve the throbbing erection hanging thick and heavy between my legs.

I'm desperate for a release, but fight back the urge to take myself in hand. Despite the hormonal monster Isobel has managed to bring out inside me, I'm not an impulsive, reckless teenager anymore. I have these desires, but I don't have to act on them. Thinking these things about Isobel is violation enough, but to act on them would be unconscionable.

Her fucking body, though... Christ, I'm only human.

If I had to come up with a list of every physical feature I'm most attracted to in a woman, Isobel would miraculously, *horribly*, possess them all. She's a walking, talking embodiment of my most wicked, sordid fantasies, and I'm not strong enough to resist. My hand drifts to grip my cock, and my forehead thuds against the tile wall of the shower.

I surrender.

"Can I touch it, Daddy?" whispers Isobel, her small breasts bare and pink nipples pebbled beneath my gaze. Cute and fucking sexy at the same time. She's standing in here with me, bathing suit in a heap on the bathroom floor, water streaming over her perfect curves.

I grunt, fighting to think of *anything* else, but I'm too far gone. I can't see anything but her.

Gripping my shaft, I begin to work myself slowly as my eyes squeeze shut, surrendering. It's just a fantasy. I might be a dirty old man, but I'm not hurting anyone. I'll get this, *her*, out of my system.

"Yes, sweetheart. You can touch it." I lean back against the shower wall, watching as her hand wraps around my shaft, stroking me up and down. I'm so thick there's a gap between her thumb and fingers, and I groan, imagining how good it will feel to have her sweet pink hole stretched around my dick. A drop of precum gathers at my slit, and Isobel drops to her knees, licking it away with a happy little moan.

She likes what she does to me, likes giving just as much as I like taking. That side of me has been sleeping for a long time, but seeing her like this makes me think things, want things...

I weave my fingers into her hair and guide her mouth over my length, thrusting lazily. "That's it." I grunt when her hands come up to grip the base of my shaft, stroking in time with my thrusts. Already my balls are tightening, ready to spill a full load down her throat, but I'm nowhere near finished with her yet.

Pulling her head back, I gaze down at the beautiful girl kneeling in front of me, her puffy lips parted and eyebrows knit together in worry. "Did I do something wrong?" she asks self-consciously.

I smirk, pulling her to her feet and turning us before pressing her back against the shower wall.

The room is steaming up around us, and hot water cascades over our bodies. I take her breasts in my hands, teasing her hard little nipples. "Not at all. You were doing very well, making me feel so good." Her breath catches at my praise, and, fuck, I love that. Against her belly, my cock grows impossibly longer. "I'm going to fuck you now, Isobel. It's going to be a tight fit, and you're going to be a little tender tomorrow, but we'll go nice and slow."

She gazes up at me with wide, trusting eyes, her arms twining around my neck. "I want you, Daddy."

She's fucking breathtaking. Every inch of her is smooth and tight and too fucking young for me. I can't stop, though. I won't, not when she's looking at me like that. Slipping my hand between us, I cup her bare sex. Impossibly soft skin, sticky with arousal, greets my touch, and it's all I can do not to bend her over and fill her right now.

I hold myself back, though, determined to get her ready. Not taking my eyes off her face, I slip a single finger into her opening, groaning at how tightly her walls grip me. I've never felt anything like it, and I can't resist adding a second finger, fucking her slowly as she writhes against me, arching her back to take more.

"Daddy," she whines, her fingers biting my shoulders. "Judah, I need you, please."

I'm not waiting anymore, not when it's so clear that we both need this. Leaning forward, I grip her thighs and lift her into a better position, her sex open and unguarded against my cock. She sucks in a ragged breath as I grip myself, guiding the fat head to press against her entrance. I should have fingered her for longer, stretched her out and got her ready, but it's too late now. I'm nearly out of my mind with desire and the need to fuck my cum into her as deeply as possible.

"Daddy—" Her words become a sharp cry as I thrust into her and—

"Fuck!" My roar echoes off the bathroom walls as I come, long, thick spurts hitting the marble wall as my body seizes with pleasure. It goes on and on, the most powerful orgasm I've had in years. When the last of it finally fades away, I don't feel the relief I normally do.

Like scratching the area right beside an unbearable itch, it wasn't quite what I needed.

SUBJECT: DAY 2: ITINERARY OVERVIEW

Hello Everyone!

Now that (almost) everyone has arrived, we have decided to go ahead with our first vacation activity, sailing, and our boat will be captained by the multi-talented Dr. John Bradley!

9:00 a.m. - Meet at Resort Harbor. Please dress comfortably, wear non-slip shoes, and remember sunscreen! We will have lunch, drinks, and an early dinner on board, but please have breakfast prior. See attached link for a Google Drive document including all the resort's food options. (**Food & Drink Guide**)

We should be arriving back no later than 5:00 p.m.

See you all on board!

Evie & Reuben

five

ISOBEL

REUBEN'S MOTHER looks like she belongs on a reality show about rich housewives.

Despite getting off a plane sometime in the middle of the night and Evie's itinerary ordering us all here by nine in the morning, Kennedy Lucas breezes onto the dock where we're standing with a full face of makeup, a designer bag hanging from her arm, and professionally colored blonde hair that doesn't seem to be the slightest bit affected by the tropical humidity. She's followed by her slightly shorter husband, whose gold watch is glinting in the bright morning sun. I watch as she points to us in the distance, her dazzlingly white smile visible even from here, and he nods obligingly.

Judah still hasn't appeared, but the rest of us are dressed casually for a day at sea. Determined *not* to dress for his eyes, I wore a loose t-shirt and shorts, but I can't help regretting it now that I see Kennedy's expensive-looking romper. Not that I'm in competition with his ex. What Judah Hale thinks about me doesn't matter.

I don't *want* him to be attracted to me.

I would expect a woman like Kennedy to be a nightmare to my mother, but they embrace warmly, exclaiming that they can't believe their babies are getting married while Evie and Reuben linger by their side, ignored.

"And this must be your sister, Isobel?" Kennedy asks Evie, smiling warmly at me when she finally tears herself away from my mother. "Another future Doctor Bradley?"

Evie laughs. "Obviously."

Hopefully. Though my inbox was still empty when I refreshed it half a dozen times before coming here.

"She'll be getting her acceptance from Weston Med any day now," Reuben tells her, shooting me a grin. He seems to be a lot like Judah, amiable and kind, the kind of person you can't help but like. "Isobel, this is my mother, Kennedy, and her husband, Tom. Their son, my brother, Nolan, will be arriving the day after tomorrow. He had a work emergency."

Kennedy lets out a tinkling laugh. "I'm always telling him to work less, but he never listens. Goodness, Isobel, you're such a beauty. Just like your sister."

"Oh, um, thank you?"

She's already moved on to hugging my father and reminding him he promised to participate in her charity event next month. And, like I can sense him coming, I turn just in time to see Judah rounding the corner onto the dock. Like most of us, he's dressed in a t-shirt and shorts, his graying hair still damp from the shower. As he draws nearer, I see he has a book tucked under his arm.

"Good morning, everyone." His low voice resonates deep inside me, and my stomach flutters, even as I shrink back toward the coolers to get out of everyone's way. "Kennedy, Tom, good to see you both."

I don't know how long he and Kennedy have been

divorced, but for her to have an adult son with another man, it must be a long time. There doesn't appear to be any animosity between them either, and I watch out of the corner of my eye as he kisses his ex-wife's cheek and shakes hands with her husband before finally turning to greet my parents with noticeably less warmth.

Huh.

Is there some history there that I don't know about?

"We should get going!" Evie calls over everyone's heads, gesturing toward today's scheduled family bonding activity: the huge, sleek white sailboat floating alongside the dock. My father tried to teach Evie and me to sail as kids, though between boarding school and his schedule, I remember the family boat sat unused in the marina for years at a time, and we never quite picked up on it. Dad is in his element, though, bossing everyone around as we get on board, and I have no desire to get in his way.

I settle as far away from where everyone is sitting on the stern as possible, leaning against the cockpit with my legs stretched out on the deck as the sounds of laughter and happy chatter carry over to me in the wind. It doesn't take long for the sails to unfurl and for Dad to steer the boat out of the resort's little harbor toward open water.

I have to admit, this feels pretty wonderful. The anxiety that's gripped me for weeks is ebbing away the further we get from land, and I lean my head back with a sigh. I should probably sit back with everyone else, have a few drinks, and spend time with my family. That was my plan, after all. Since getting here, though, I've felt so much more removed from them than I remember being the last time we were together. I don't know what to say, how to act, or how to begin breaking into that closed Evie-Mom-Dad circle.

After I get into medical school, it will be better. They'll

be pleased. We'll have things to talk about, places and life experiences in common. I bet this time next year, I'll be a whole new person.

Sighing, I reach into my bag and pull out the mystery novel I bought at the airport, sliding my sunglasses down off the top of my head and cracking open the brand-new paperback. I can't remember the last time I read a book that had nothing to do with pharmacology, biology, or chemistry. I only have a few weeks before my last undergraduate semester starts, and detaching myself from reality sounds pretty good right now.

I've barely made it past the first paragraph when motion out of the corner of my eye makes me look up sharply. Judah is standing over me, his own book grasped in his hand, and I realize with a little jolt that it's the same as mine.

"Sorry, I thought you were below," he says quietly, gesturing back toward the stern. I expect him to leave, but he doesn't. "I, ah. I wanted to touch base about yesterday."

Shit. *Yesterday.* I thought we were pretending that didn't happen. I apologized. What more does he want?

Behind us, I hear Kennedy's and my mother's laughter and glance uneasily over my shoulder. Even though talking about this is the last thing in the world I want to do, I still find myself scooting over to make room for him to sit beside me. Judah's eyes flair with surprise, but he doesn't hesitate, folding himself down onto the deck so that his much longer legs are stretched out beside mine. We're sitting at a perfectly respectful distance apart, but I'm still hyperaware of where his body is in proximity to mine.

I'm determined not to look at him, but as soon as he says, "I wasn't upset about you not liking the wine at dinner." I'm so taken aback that I can't help looking around.

He's looking at me with his brow furrowed, like this has been really bothering him and he's seizing the first opportunity he can to clear the air. I was expecting a hushed, urgent request to never tell a soul about the first time we met, not for him actually to care what I think of him.

Something knots inside me as Judah plows on, his voice low, "I was angry at how your mother spoke to you, *nothing* else. I hope you can forgive me for not being clear on that. I'm sorry."

Why does this whole interaction make me want to cry?

I turn back to face the boat's bow, the wind on my face. "I'm sorry too. I'm sure I made a face."

Judah's answering chuckle settles low in my belly, and my core clenches. Why is it that everything this man does is attractive to me?

"You did," he admits. "But you didn't order the wine, Isobel. Your opinion wasn't asked. You have every right not to enjoy it."

Damn it.

I find myself willing away the burning in my eyes. I know he's right, but twenty-three years of gnawing inadequacy and self-doubt, fueled by my parents' steadfast indifference, has pretty much trained me to look for my own fault in any given situation. It's a little uncomfortable for someone to see that and call me on it. I was so taken aback by the rush that came the first time I saw this man's face that all my usual defenses went down, and now I don't know how to put them back up.

"Isobel?"

Confident I'm not about to embarrass myself further by crying, I turn back to look at him and lift the book resting in my lap. "We should probably read these, right?" My voice sounds falsely cheery and casual. "Unless you want to go back there and play twenty questions, rare disease edition."

Judah's lips split in a crooked grin, the wind ruffling his graying hair and his eyes shining behind his glasses. "Don't tell me that's what the Bradley family played on road trips instead of *I Spy*."

I have to press my lips together to keep myself from grinning back at him. "Not a road trip kind of family. Though I remember some pretty intense rounds of Weston Medical School trivia on the way to Rosh Hashanah services."

His answering bark of laughter makes me giggle too. Our family members are standing just a few yards behind us, but I can hardly hear their voices over the wind carrying the boat. I feel better than I have in a long time and allow my eyes to drift back down to my book. Out of the corner of my eye, I see Judah open his, and we lapse into silence, reading side by side.

There have been lots of long silences in my life, but this one doesn't feel lonely. Judah must realize we're reading the same book at some point because he says, "The bridge in this chapter is going to be significant, don't you think?"

My lips twitch, though I keep my eyes down. "Definitely."

Reuben finds us not long later, grinning when he sees our matching books. "I wondered if you two had fallen off somewhere. Is this a book club?"

"Apparently." Judah chuckles. "I picked it up at the airport."

"Me too," I admit, smiling. "You can have my copy when I'm done. We can discuss the book's underlying themes at your wedding reception."

Reuben tilts his head back and laughs. "Sounds like fun, though I'm worried the cake cutting and first dance will be distracting." Evie appears at his side, her hair less tidy than usual from the wind and her cheeks flushed. She looks happier than I've seen her in a long time. "Dad and Isobel accidentally started a book club," he informs her. "Should we join?"

"Absolutely." My sister grins, sitting cross-legged on the deck across from us. "No, seriously. Can we do that? Virtual family book club once a month?"

I nod immediately, my cheeks aching from smiling so big. "I'd love that. I don't read enough."

"None of us do, I bet." Reuben sighs, sitting down next to his fiancée and kissing her temple. Behind them, I can see other boats dotted over the turquoise sea around us and a beautiful stretch of coastline in the distance. "You'll know soon enough, Isobel. Medical school is not for the faint of heart."

And just like that, all my newfound peace is gone. My stomach churning, I look away from the group, trying to fight back the urge to vomit. I'm not going to puke in front of them. *God,* we were having a nice moment...

It's no use.

Scrambling to the side of the boat, I lean over the railing, staring down into the waves for a fraction of a second before my stomach rolls and I heave again, vomiting the remains of my breakfast right into the water. I'm only alone for a second before someone has gathered my hair back, and a hand is rubbing soothing circles over my back.

"You're alright. Get it all out," Judah murmurs. My eyes burn with tears of humiliation as another wave of nausea hits me, and I heave again.

"Dad!" Evie calls loudly behind me. "Take us back to the resort! Isobel is seasick!"

I squeeze my eyes shut, panting. The moment I'm sure it's over, I scramble to my feet. "I'm fine," I assure Reuben and Evie, not daring to look at Judah. "I'm really okay." Kennedy, Tom, and Mom have all appeared, staring at me, and my chest tightens with embarrassment. "I'm fine," I repeat, shaking my head.

Mom's lips pinch. "You never used to have a problem on boats. Did you have anything alcoholic to drink at breakfast?"

"No." I pull my water bottle out of my bag and take a long sip, swishing the water around in my mouth to get rid of the foul taste. I want to disappear. *What is wrong with me?*

"I think we should head back. *Now*," Judah tells the group, his voice deep and laced with authority.

"No." I won't ruin the first outing Evie planned because I'm a basket case. "No, I'm okay. I'm just going to lay down below."

Nobody stops me as I gather my things and slip back around the cockpit. I pass Dad at the wheel, whose signature disappointed frown is firmly in place. "Let's skip the mimosas at breakfast tomorrow, Isobel."

It was orange juice, but they've clearly made up their minds about me. Who am I to argue?

* * *

I sleep for a long time, not waking up until Evie comes down to rub my shoulder and softly tell me we're back at the resort.

On the deck, everyone looks windswept and tan, wearing wide, easy smiles and making jokes about the

45

terrible sandwiches as we file off onto the dock. All except Judah, who looks more like he's been attending a funeral than spending a day at sea with his future in-laws and his son.

"Feeling better, Isobel?" asks Kennedy kindly when I step off beside her, and I have to rip my eyes from her ex-husband's ass to look back at her.

"I'm okay, thank you. Just seasick."

Evie disembarks next and stands beside me, looping her arm through mine. "So, no word from Weston?"

My stomach churns. "No. Not yet."

I'm sure we look like any ordinary pair of sisters from the outside. Maybe to Evie, we are, but even though connecting with her has always been something I've wanted desperately, now that she's trying, I just feel... scared. She doesn't know me and, as silly as it sounds, I can't help the nagging, childish worry that she won't like me when she does.

Evie nods thoughtfully, her brow furrowed. "I'm sure you'll get in no problem. Maybe I'll drive to Boston once you're settled and show you my favorite haunts from med school."

"I'd love that." We walk together to the end of the dock and turn back to see Dad, Tom, Reuben, and Judah unloading fishing gear and coolers while Mom and Kennedy talk off to the side.

"I know they're not easy on you." I look up, my eyes widening in surprise. Evie has never criticized our parents or said a negative word about them, at least not to me. She's looking at me now with a sad, almost mournful expression. "I just want you to know you can talk to me. As a fellow victim of Bradley pressure-cooker parenting."

I nod, but don't say anything. It seems shitty to admit,

even to myself, but I don't think I completely trust her. I can't imagine us having the kind of relationship where we can bitch about Mom and Dad, especially since they treat her like she walks on water. "Okay. Thank you," I whisper, and I see Evie's shoulders fall just a little.

My eyes drift, almost unwillingly, to Judah. He's standing with his arms crossed over his broad chest, talking to Tom. "Do you like him?" I ask suddenly, looking back at her. "Judah, I mean. What do you think of him?"

Evie tilts her head, considering. "I do. I think I do, anyway. We haven't spent a ton of time together. Reuben looks up to him a lot, though. And his professional reputation is excellent."

"Do you know if he got married again after Kennedy?"

That prompts a startled laugh from Evie. "What on Earth made you think of that?"

"Just curious." I give a noncommittal little shrug, trying to look casually interested instead of desperate for the information.

I'm not sure I pull it off because Evie's eyes are glued to my face when she responds. "No, he never got married again. Reuben's told me he doesn't date much either. A few girlfriends here and there, but nobody who stuck around long."

I refuse to consider why her words make me feel lighter than I have in days.

six

JUDAH

"I'M glad we're doing this."

Reuben leads the way through the crowded resort restaurant to the bar. There's nothing on Evie's schedule for tonight, giving everyone a chance to relax after a long day on the water, so I seized my opportunity to grab a few minutes alone with my son.

Today was, frankly, brutal. In addition to the obsessive attraction, Isobel seems to bring out a near-feral level of protectiveness. Watching from the outside as she struggles, trying to force herself to want things she doesn't for the sake of people who treat her like dirt, is agonizing. We're only two days into this trip, and already the restraint I'm employing to keep myself from saying something to Caroline and John is wearing thin.

As we sit down at the bar, Reuben looks over at me. "Something's bothering you."

I don't deny it. "John and Caroline... Isobel."

Apparently, I don't need to explain further because Reuben nods, his expression growing tight too. "I know."

"Is this normal?" I ask desperately, dropping my voice

to ensure we aren't overheard. "You've been around them as a family more than I have. Is it always like this?"

Reuben sighs. "I *haven't* spent much time with them as a family. Isobel goes to college in Chicago. She doesn't come home much—"

"Do you blame her?" I snap, immediately on the defensive. Reuben gives me a look, and I nod in mute apology.

"Anyway." He shakes his head, grimacing. "I convinced Evie to start therapy a few months ago, and while it's helping a bit, she has a long way to go. It hasn't been a cakewalk for her either."

I'm sure it hasn't, but the difference is that Evie loves medicine. I saw it in her eyes when we talked about her career. She's passionate about it, excited. Isobel looks like she's being marched to the gallows whenever it's brought up. "You both need to ease up on the medical school talk," I tell him warningly. "She doesn't want to go. Maybe if Evie talked to her—"

"How do you know that?" asks Reuben sharply, his eyebrows knitted together in surprised confusion.

My son is intelligent, but he can't pick up on a hint if it hits him in the face. "She *threw up* the moment you mentioned it today, Reuben. We sat there reading for an hour. She was fine, *happy* even."

He opens his mouth, looking guilty. Then the bartender appears to take our orders, and we both fall silent. The restaurant is packed, and when the man leaves to get our beers, I look around to make sure none of the Bradley family members have chosen this same spot for a late-night drink.

"Listen," Reuben cautions me quietly. "Don't rock the boat, Dad. I know there are a lot of fucked-up dynamics at play, but Isobel is an adult. I'll tell Evie to speak with her, but that's all we can do. I know John and Caroline are—"

"Assholes?" I suggest a bit too loudly, and Reuben gives me an exasperated look.

"I was going to say *limited.*"

The bartender leaves two bottles before us, and I lean back on my stool, taking a long drink.

When Reuben continues, he looks weary. "Evie has a lot of guilt surrounding Isobel. She doesn't think she's been a very good sister. It's a sensitive subject. There are things I'm not going to tell you because they're not my business, and I don't think Isobel would thank me for spreading it around, but for the love of god, please just keep all this to yourself. Don't confront the Bradleys."

His words have me curious as hell, but god, he's a good kid, a good *man.* "They deserve to have someone call them on this."

"Maybe," he concedes. "But I would like to get through this week and marry the woman I love *without* a shitload of family drama. Can you help me with that?"

My stomach knots with guilt. I've been so preoccupied and worried about Isobel, I haven't thought about the position I'd be putting Reuben in if I were to get involved in the dysfunctional mess that his future wife was born into. He's right, there's bound to be a lot I don't know, and while John and Caroline's treatment of their daughters makes me sick, it doesn't change the fact that it's none of my business.

Whatever attraction I feel for Isobel, I have no claim on her. She isn't mine to protect, to advocate for, or defend. I'm her sister's father-in-law. *That's it.*

I'm here for Reuben, to support him and see him get married.

"Okay," I hear myself agree quietly, even though it tears me apart. "I just..." I shake my head, my throat tightening as the words I want to say fall away. "Okay."

Reuben winces. "I don't want you to think I'm turning a blind eye or that I don't give a damn. This isn't the time to start working through this shit, and it's not my place *or yours*. I'll talk to Evie, though, see if she can find a moment to talk to Isobel about medical school."

On the bar beside his hand, Reuben's phone chimes with a text notification. He picks it up, frowning at the screen.

"Everything alright?"

He grimaces, thumbs already flying over the screen. "Evie is freaking out. Apparently, the lady coordinating the flowers from the mainland lost our order. She wants to get over to her shop before they close, but we're supposed to meet with the resort's kitchen manager about the food for the wedding."

"I'll go," I hear myself offer. I don't know the first thing about flowers, but knowing my future daughter-in-law, she'll have very clear instructions for me to follow. "To the florist, I mean. I'll sort it out while you two meet the kitchen manager."

His thumbs pause, and he frowns at me. "You're sure? I'm sure it'll take ages."

I snort, taking another sip of my beer. "What else do I have to do?"

Why the fuck do I instantly think of Isobel naked beneath me when I say those words?

Reuben is apparently checking this solution with Evie because, after another few text exchanges, he nods at me. "Batter up. Thanks, Dad."

"No problem." I hold a hand up to signal the bartender for a check just as Reuben's phone chimes again, and he chuckles at whatever Evie says.

"She says she's asking Isobel to go too unless you'd

51

rather I send Mom or Caroline to keep you company?" He grins, and I make a strained attempt at a casual laugh.

I can't think of any objection I could raise to this plan with Reuben, but I can't think of anything more dangerous than spending time alone with Isobel Bradley.

* * *

"Okay, so they're supposed to be *white* orchids, not pink."

The woman across the counter stares at me, clearly bemused, and bites back in accented English, "The order said pink."

I let out a long, slow breath, willing myself not to get frustrated. "I thought you didn't have the order, which is why we're here?" I gesture between myself and Issy, who is standing beside me. Her lips are pinched, and she looks like she's on the verge of throwing the nearest vase at this woman's head. We've been in this shop for forty-five minutes, following a painful thirty-minute drive here with me trying to make conversation with her while she made noncommittal noises in response.

I'm still not confident the florist even knows which wedding she's discussing. When the woman leaves again to check the back, Issy's head drops back, staring at the ceiling in a silent show of frustration.

She looks beautiful today, with her hair loose around her shoulders and wearing a plain black sundress which makes her skin look flawless and creamy. We met in the lobby early this morning, and I couldn't help but hope for a sighting of the version of her I've glimpsed when we're alone. So far, I've been disappointed. She didn't mean for me to see so much yesterday, and now her guard is up.

I should let the walls stand after my talk with Reuben last night, but it's fucking eating at me.

"Are you looking forward to the hike later?"

It's a pretty weak attempt at small talk, and I'm not entirely surprised that she doesn't bite, just smiles weakly and nods. "Yes."

Look at me.

Talk to me.

The shopkeeper returns, brandishing a piece of paper and speaking in rapid French to someone on the phone. When she hangs up, she nods. "Okay, all set."

I have to press my lips together to keep myself from laughing out loud at the outraged, furious expression on Issy's face. "Come on." I press my hand to the small of her back and guide us back onto the bustling street before she loses it. "We got what we wanted."

"How are you so calm about this?" she bursts out furiously, glaring over our shoulders at the woman. "That was infuriating."

I shrug. It was, but it hardly seems important now. I'm far too interested in the fiery, annoyed woman at my side to have room in my brain for anything else. "Are you hungry?" I nod toward a shop selling sandwiches that look incredible. "I don't know about you, but I'm already sick of gourmet fish for breakfast, lunch, and dinner."

"We need to get back," she clips, shaking her head. "Everyone is supposed to meet for the hike at noon."

I check my watch. "There's plenty of time."

Not giving her the opportunity to come up with another objection, I steer us toward the shop, where a short line of tourists and locals are waiting for their turn to order. "There's a place like this around the corner from the hospital where I practice," I tell her quietly, letting my hand fall from her back and missing the contact immediately. "One of my patients and her husband own it. She brought me a sandwich at one of her prenatal appointments, and I swear the woman knew exactly what she was doing because now I go every chance I get. I didn't tell her I was going out of town, so I'm sure they'll send out a search party when I don't turn up for a week straight."

Issy is silent for so long that I think I've hit another stone wall, but my heart leaps when she looks up at me tentatively, her brow furrowed. "Is that weird? Seeing patients outside of work?"

I grin, not at her question, but because she asked one at all. "No. I like it a lot, actually. Running into an old patient in the supermarket with the wild four-year-old I delivered is amazing. That's the only thing I don't like about this specialty—not getting to follow my patients past postpartum. Do you, ah, like kids?" The question is casual—it shouldn't matter if she does or doesn't—but my heart still hammers against my rib cage in the time it takes her to respond.

Her eyes turn down as though she's confessing something embarrassing. "I, um, actually volunteer at a nonprofit daycare back in Chicago. I'm not a teacher, but I go in three times a week to read to the kids and do craft projects with them."

Her parents think she volunteers at the hospital. They asked about it on our first night here. I don't know what makes me happier: that she confided in me or that she spends her free time playing with children from low-income families so their parents can work.

I'm supposed to be playing it cool, but I can't help my smile, feeling lighter than I have in days. "That's amazing. You like it, I assume?" She nods, and though she keeps her eyes trained forward, I can see a subtle dip in her bottom lip, like she's biting it to keep herself from smiling. She does it a lot.

Without warning, I'm filled with a vicious, burning hatred for Caroline and John Bradley. What was it like to grow up as Issy? For her to see her parents openly adore Evie while being treated with cold disapproval and disinterest? Those people made her afraid, disconnected her from happiness, and did their damn best to crush her spirit. It's still there, though, shoved down and hidden away maybe, but somehow, miraculously, alive.

What I'm feeling for her now has nothing to do with the fierce, instinctual attraction I've felt for her from that first moment on the plane. It's tamer but no less potent, and I can't put a word to it for the life of me. Everything I've felt with Isobel is brand new but this... *shit*.

I'm so incredibly fucked.

FROM: E.BRADLEY@COLUMBIAMED.COM

TO: C.HOLMESBRADLEY@NYCMED.COM, JBRADLEY@NYCMED.COM,
R.HALE@COLUMBIAMED.COM, J.HALE@CDC.GOV,
KENNEDY@LUCASREALTY.COM, NOLAN@LUCAS REALTY.COM,
TOM@LUCASREALTY.COM, I.BRADLEY@UCHICAGO.EDU

SUBJECT: DAY 3: ITINERARY OVERVIEW (PLEASE NOTE CHANGE!!!)

Good Afternoon Family!

We had so much fun sailing with everyone yesterday! Unfortunately, some wedding planning issues have arisen, so we will have to leave for our scheduled hike at 1 p.m. instead of 11 a.m. It's a little bit of a drive, and we have dinner reservations at an off-resort restaurant on the way home, so please make sure you are on time.

12:45 p.m. - Meet in Resort Lobby
1:00 p.m. - Depart for Hike
6:00 p.m. - Reservations at local seafood restaurant (link for menu).

We should arrive back no later than 8 P.M. A special shout-out to Judah and Isobel for saving the day and taking care of our very annoying florist issue!

Evie & Reuben

FROM: E.BRADLEY@COLUMBIAMED.COM

TO: C.HOLMESBRADLEY@NYCMED.COM, JBRADLEY@NYCMED.COM,
R.HALE@COLUMBIAMED.COM, J.HALE@CDC.GOV,
KENNEDY@LUCASREALTY.COM, NOLAN@LUCAS REALTY.COM,
TOM@LUCASREALTY.COM, I.BRADLEY@UCHICAGO.EDU

SUBJECT: DAY 3: ITINERARY OVERVIEW (ANOTHER CHANGE!)

So sorry for the confusion, everyone!

I was informed by the resort personnel that the restaurant we planned on attending does NOT have a vegetarian option (as they advertise). As several members of our party require that, I have canceled the reservation. Luckily the resort was able to accommodate us at La Grille. Please find the corrected itinerary below.

12:45 p.m. - Meet in Resort Lobby
1:00 p.m. - Depart for Hike
6:15 p.m. - Reservations at La Grille (located in east corner of the resort)

Evie & Reuben

seven

ISOBEL

DESPITE JUDAH'S assurances we have plenty of time, we arrive back at the hotel with only ten minutes to spare before meeting everyone for the hike.

He didn't keep up his attempts to get me talking while we sat side by side on a bench eating smoked chicken sandwiches, and I hate that it makes me disappointed instead of relieved. I should be happy he's getting the hint, that he's sick of my prickly, unsociable vibe and has decided I'm more trouble than I'm worth.

I power walk back to my bungalow to change, leaving Judah to wait for everyone in the lobby. I take the time to smooth my hair back into a neat ponytail for my mother's benefit and, out of habit, refresh my email.

Nothing. Still nothing.

Cursing when I see the time, I hurry over to the closet to get my hiking boots. I'm held up yet again when one of the laces snaps, and by the time I finally arrive back in the resort's lobby—ten minutes past our scheduled departure time—I find it completely devoid of Bradley or Hale family members.

Trying in vain to fight back the wave of anxiety I get from moments like this, I collapse into one of the sleek white armchairs clustered around the lobby. They seriously left without me? I have my phone on me. They could have texted, called...

"Isobel?" My heart leaps as I turn in my seat to face Judah, who is standing just behind my chair dressed in the same shorts and plain white t-shirt that fit him so well it should be criminal. How can he walk around looking like that and expect anyone to get anything done?

I never understood the point of the extra n's tacked on to the end of the word *damnnnn* until I met him.

I look around the lobby for the rest of our families, but he's alone. "Did you miss them too?"

Judah smiles wryly and shakes his head. "There was some debate on whether we should wait for you. I said I would and take you myself." There's a hint of disapproval in his tone that suggests he thinks they *all* should have waited, and my whole body feels suddenly warm in a way that has nothing to do with the resort's tropical climate.

"You didn't have to do that."

He shakes his head, still looking annoyed, and walks over to take the seat across from mine. "We were doing something for the wedding, Isobel. They *all* should have waited."

"Surgeons aren't known for their flexibility." I huff, playing with the hem of my shorts as I try not to stare at the way the sleeves of his t-shirt stretch just a little over his biceps.

I really noticed it at dinner the first night we were here, but it strikes me again that Judah doesn't seem to have a problem with just... looking at me. He doesn't glance around the room, at his phone, or at people around me. It's a little disarming, but I kind of like it too. I don't have to wonder if he's listening.

Leaning forward, Judah smiles slightly, his eyes searching my face. "So, I wanted to ask you. Why medical school?"

I blink in surprise. Of all the things I expected to come out of his mouth, that wasn't one of them. Did Weston send him as an undercover admissions agent or something? "You're a physician. Do you regret it?"

"Of course not. It's not for everyone, though. Obviously."

"It's for me. I'm a good student," I bite back, suddenly defensive. Does he think I'm not up to the task? My stomach drops to the floor. He barely even knows me. How could he possibly make that judgment? Is there something about my face that screams *"incompetent idiot"*? I'm pretty confident that most of my family thinks that's exactly what I am. I've known that for a long time, so why does it sting so much that Judah does too?

His eyes flash. "I didn't say that you weren't. You're clearly intelligent, Isobel. I didn't mean to suggest otherwise—"

"We should go if we're going to catch up to them." I stand up quickly, hitching my backpack over my shoulder, desperate to leave this conversation behind. "Did you return the resort's courtesy car or—"

When I begin to turn toward the entrance of the resort, a large, warm hand closes on my wrist. My head whips around automatically, staring back into Judah's bright-blue eyes, which are widened in surprise, as though he's just as surprised as I am to find his hand on me.

"I'm sorry." His hand drops away immediately, but just like when he held my hand on the airport shuttle and when he touched my back at the flower shop this morning, the warmth of it lingers on my skin. "I realize how that might have sounded as though I were... I wasn't doubting you. You'll make an excellent physician if that's what you want."

I square my jaw defiantly and want more than anything to spit out that it's the most important thing in my life. That I eat, sleep, and breathe it the way he and my family do, but I can't quite manage to say the words. Clearing my throat, I nod in silent acceptance of his apology. "It *is* what I want."

What is it about this man that makes me incapable of lying my ass off? I've been doing it all my life—to myself, my parents, and the whole world. So why can't I open my mouth and tell my sister's future father-in-law that I want to be a doctor, that I want it more than anything, and I doodle little stethoscopes on all my school papers?

Judah's eyes search my face, and after what feels like an age, he finally nods. "Okay."

"Okay," I agree, folding my arms over my chest and trying not to look like I'm on the verge of unraveling.

He gives me a smile that I don't return, hating that my heart flutters at how the act deepens the little wrinkles that appear at the corners of his eyes. "Let's get going, then. I picked up some bottled water for both of us."

"I'm actually going to head back to my bungalow."

Judah's face falls, and I feel a sick lurch of regret. This man, this sweet, considerate, amazing man, is going to walk around all day feeling like shit because he thinks he offended me when in reality, this begins and ends with me. The only thing Judah did wrong was try to be nice to me. As if I needed more proof that I have no business wanting him the way I do.

The thought makes my heart ache, and my fingernails bite into my palms.

"Isobel," he starts to say, but I'm already backing away, desperate to get as far away as possible.

Every instinct I have is screaming—*RUN!*—and for once this week, I have no intention of ignoring it. "I'll see you at dinner. I think Evie's having the kitchen prepare our great-grandmother's kugel recipe, so that should be... um, interesting."

I hate him. I hate how good my name sounds on his lips and how he *won't stop looking at me*. I don't want his concern or his care or that hint of something deeper I don't dare acknowledge. I don't even know him. We met three days ago. Yet in that time, he's managed to make me completely lose my grip. Why is he doing this to me? Why won't he just *stop*?

Outside, the humidity is already starting to descend on the resort, and I move so fast that my back is sticky by the time I make it back to my bungalow. Just for something to do other than think about what transpired between me and Judah, I flip open my laptop again and refresh my email. I'm sure it didn't arrive in the past five minutes, but... *It did*. Right there, between a promotional email for a t-shirt company and an automated reminder I have a dentist appointment next week, an unopened message from the Weston University Admissions Office.

Oh my god.

My fingers feel clumsy and awkward as I open it and click the link provided, my heart beating wildly.

I might not get in, I remind myself for the hundredth time. I'm prepared for that. Nepotism is a powerful thing, but Weston probably gets hundreds of legacy applications every year. There's no guarantee. At the end of the day, they aren't going to waste a spot on an alumni's kid who might end up washing out. I've never been a naturally incredible student like Evie. I don't have as many references as she did or—

Dear Miss Bradley,

We regret to inform you that you are not among the applicants who have been selected for this year's—

My hands fall away from the computer, and I stumble away from the table, blood rushing in my ears so loud that it drowns out the ocean outside.

I didn't get in.

I really didn't get in.

Right there below the crimson letterhead is undeniable proof of what I've suspected all along: I really am just as much of an outsider in my family as I always thought. Four generations of Doctor Bradleys have gone to Weston, each of them somehow more successful than the last, and I am the weak branch that's snapped off the family tree, doomed to rot on the ground below.

I don't remember sitting down, but I am, right in the middle of the floor in the stunning villa my *doctor* parents paid for so I can attend my *doctor* sister's wedding to her *doctor* husband while I lust after his *doctor* father. What is wrong with me? How could I have messed this up? All I needed to do was be even *mildly* competent, and surely my last name would have done the rest. But, no. Weston realized what my parents and my sister know, what Judah knows, and what I've been feebly trying to deny to myself my whole life. I am *not* a Bradley.

Some part of me realizes what's happening. I've had a panic attack before; I know what it means when the room begins to spin like this, when the air I'm breathing doesn't seem to be making it into my burning lungs, and my whole body feels like it's been dunked in ice. Knowing it doesn't help, though. It just reinforces the horrible thoughts churning rapidly through my mind. My parents don't have panic attacks, nor does my sister. Just me. Me, the failure. Me, the disappointment. Me, the one who tried and tried but who isn't quite good enough.

I can hear knocking somewhere in the distance, but it seems so far away that it doesn't really register. Or it doesn't until I hear a panicked male voice yell my name. I still can't look around or do anything but rock back and forth, my breaths coming in desperate, ragged gulps.

"Isobel!" The voice is closer now, and warm arms are wrapping around me, dragging me back into a big, firm chest.

Someone is seeing me like this. Someone knows. "Listen to me." A hand strokes my hair, and the male voice speaks quietly and calmly into my ear. "I need you to take a deep breath with me in. One, two..."

I try to obey. Really, I do, but it's impossible. Tears are rolling down my cheeks, my whole body is shaking, and the ragged sound I make is so pitiful it makes me cry harder. I can't even breathe right? *What is wrong with me?*

"Shhhh." He holds my body tightly against his, and he's so warm compared to me that it's almost unbearable. "You're alright. We're going to try again, okay? Deep breath in. One, two..." I manage it this time, greedily sucking in oxygen as the man holding me does the same, his chest rising and falling with mine. "Very good. *Very good.* Okay. Again, nice and slow."

I don't know how long we sit there, the man's voice in my ear calmly coaching me through breath after breath as his warmth bleeds into my cold body. At some point, I realize I'm sitting between his legs, still in the middle of the villa's floor. Bit by bit, the world comes back to me until I hear the man's voice in my ear again, smell his earthy, masculine scent, and it finally registers who is holding me.

Judah.

"You're okay." He strokes my hair, his cheek pressed against my head, speaking into my ear. "Everything's okay. I'm here. I've got you, Issy."

Issy. Nobody calls me that.

I'm so weak and exhausted that it doesn't even occur to me to argue or to try and preserve what's left of my pride. What's more, I don't remember the last time someone held me like this. The few boyfriends I've had were passing experiments, halfhearted attempts to see if another person could turn me into one of those happy girls who tell strangers on the bus she likes their outfit. They couldn't, and either I got tired of pretending, or he got tired of trying to connect with me, and we went our separate ways. I didn't love any of them, not even close. They didn't hold me the way Judah is right now, or if they did, it didn't make me feel the way I do now.

Wanted.

It takes a long time for my breathing to finally even out and my heartbeat to slow, but Judah doesn't let me go. He keeps stroking my hair and murmuring quiet, comforting words in my ear.

"I didn't get in," I finally confess, my voice strained and emotionless. I'm so tired, so drained, that it's too much just to get the words out. My eyes flutter shut, and I melt even deeper into Judah's warmth, feeling his chest rising and falling in time with mine.

Judah doesn't tell me that there are other schools, or that everything is going to work out in the end, or that I can try again next year. The last thing I hear as my exhausted body finally surrenders to sleep is his gentle voice in my ear, rough with emotion. "I'm here."

JUDAH

ISOBEL DOESN'T TURN up for dinner.

I suffer through the meal with my fists clenched beneath the table, more hatred than I've ever felt directed right at the people across the table from me who are eating their dinner and drinking their wine without a care in the world. Every time they look at Evie with warm pride or brag about her accomplishments to Kennedy or Tom, I hear ringing in my ears, and it takes everything in me not to roar.

I can't understand it. *She's their daughter.*

Their intelligent, kind, beautiful daughter. By the looks of it, they've spent her entire life, *twenty-three years*, putting her second to her sister simply because she isn't who they want her to be. It couldn't be clearer to me that in Isobel's mind, becoming a doctor has become inextricably linked to becoming a part of her family, *to belonging.*

She's terrified of connecting to anyone, of letting a single piece of herself show. It's not a mystery why, when her parents seize any possible opportunity to point out her faults. How she reacted when she learned she didn't get into Weston makes perfect sense the more I think about it.

The whole business is so unspeakably fucked up that it's only for Reuben's sake I manage to keep myself from flipping the table and sending our shitty kugel dinner all over John and Caroline.

I can't stop thinking about how I found her—huddled on the floor, struggling to breathe, her whole body shaking. None of that was the reaction of a healthy, well-adjusted young woman experiencing disappointment. God knows what it was like growing up with these people as parents. From what Reuben has told me about Evie, it's clear she's likely struggling too.

I slip away from dinner as quickly as possible, muttering something about a headache after John calls Evie his "shining star" for the third time in half an hour, and go back to Isobel's villa to check on her. She hasn't moved an inch from where I left her hours ago, curled in the center of the massive bed, her breathing deep and measured. I still don't know what it is about this woman that draws me in so intensely, but as I linger in the doorway to her bedroom, watching her sleep, I ache to crawl into bed behind her and hold her in my arms again.

She's too young for me, I barely know her, and she's struggling with things I'm not supposed to get involved in. On the rare occasions I've imagined what it would be like to fall in love, to *really* fall in love, it wasn't like this. It wasn't a fucking battle. I want to be angry with whatever it is inside me that seems to have decided that this is the woman for me, but I'm not. Every time I get a hint of who she is beyond that stoic, cold facade, I fall harder, and a part of me knows it's already too late. I can't not feel this.

I'm exhausted, but I can't bring myself to walk the twenty yards away to my bungalow. I can't leave her, not after today. Instead, I lay back on the plush white couch and stare at the ceiling fan rotating slowly above my head.

It might have been minutes or hours, but the moon is high outside the back doors when I jerk awake at the sound of soft footsteps. My eyes find her immediately, wrapped in a sheet from the bed and staring at me through the semi-darkness.

"You're still here," Isobel says quietly, her expression unreadable.

Scrubbing a hand roughly over my face, I sit up, swinging my legs over the edge of the couch. "I left for a while. Went to dinner with... everyone." I don't know how I will get through the rest of this week when I can't even say John's and Caroline's names out loud.

Isobel must sense the anger behind my words because she sinks down at the far end of the couch, curling her knees up against her chest. "It's not their fault I wasn't accepted."

Fuck, I hate how defeated she sounds right now. "No, but it is their fault you applied in the first place. Do you *want* to be a doctor, Isobel?"

She winces. "I—"

"Because if you don't, it means sacrificing your happiness for theirs. Is that fucking fair? Is that what you would ask your children to do?" I scoff, shaking my head because I already know the answer. "How they treat you is the opposite of love, sweetheart. It's manipulative and cold. I don't know why they're like this, but they don't deserve a thing from you. So, why are you giving them your fucking life?"

Isobel's eyes drop, and I'm instantly ashamed of myself. She had a panic attack today. The last thing she needs is for me to berate her, but as soon as I open my mouth to apologize, her quiet voice comes through the shadows.

"I know it's not... normal. The way they treat me, I mean. I know I'm never going to be good enough for them, Weston or not. I guess I just thought if I checked all the items on their list, did everything Evie did, they'd finally ask themselves why they don't love me."

My heart breaks.

Before I can think better of it, I'm moving onto the floor, kneeling at her feet and gathering her face in my hands so she has no choice but to look down at me. "Issy," I murmur. "If they were capable of asking themselves that question, they would have done it a long time ago."

Tears fall over her cheeks, and I wipe them away with my thumbs, my whole body tense with the effort it takes to keep myself from gathering her in my arms again. "Tell me what you want," I plead. I will do anything for this girl. In just a few days, Isobel Bradley has become the center of my world, and, *damn me*, I don't give a fuck who she is anymore. Every instinct inside me is bellowing that this beautiful, hurt creature is meant for me, and the rest of my life hangs on the question I just asked her.

"Nobody's ever asked me that before." She gives a watery laugh. "You have some nerve, Doctor Hale."

"Issy—"

"Why do you call me that?" she demands suddenly. "Nobody else does."

Intoxicated by my new realization *that I'm doing this*, I draw my thumb over her bottom lip, blood rushing to my cock when I hear her breath catch. "Do you not like it?" She trembles, but doesn't move a muscle. We're so close together that I can smell the ocean on her skin, can see the tears clinging to her eyelashes. I'd barely have to move to kiss her, and while I want it more than anything, I know I have to do this right. Like trying to calm a scared animal, I know any sudden movements will send her scurrying back to safety.

"No," she lies, her voice throaty. "No, I don't like it."

I have to bite back a smile. "Would you like me to call you something else?" My hand moves back to tangle through her hair, pulling just enough to ensure she feels it. "Sweetheart?"

She squeaks, her eyes going wide like I just cursed at her. "*No.*"

"Baby girl?" Her legs snap together as the words leave my mouth, and *fuck* does that make me hard. It would be so goddamn easy to wedge my hands between her creamy thighs, push them back open, and not let her close them again until I've felt how wet I make her.

"Judah." She's doing her best to sound outraged, but it isn't working.

"Princess?" Issy groans and tries to squirm out of my grasp, but I hold her still, murmuring the truth softly into her ear. "I call you Issy *because* nobody else does. Maybe I want a piece of you all to myself. Did that ever occur to you?"

Her body trembles, and I press my forehead against her temple, unable to resist breathing in the salt and wind that lingers on her skin. She smells like freedom. "We can't, Judah."

We can't, not *I don't want you* or *leave me alone.*

I can work with that. She isn't pushing me away, either. Her body has relaxed into mine, and damn it, now that I know what it's like to hold her like this, how the hell am I supposed to stop?

"We'll talk about it tomorrow." Before she can stop me, I slide an arm beneath her legs and one behind her back, lifting her into my arms bridal style. She gasps, her arms flying around my neck to hold on as I get to my feet, moving carefully through the darkened living room and out the open doors to the back deck. The moon is only a few days from being full and so bright in the cloudless sky that the ocean's surface seems to glow. "Swim with me."

Her chin juts out defiantly. "Why?"

It feels incredible to hold her, but something vaguely resembling a plan is taking shape in my mind, and I need to follow through. Carefully, I set her down on the deck beside me. "It will help you sleep." I pull my shirt over my head and let it fall to the deck while she watches, her eyes wide and locked on my body.

I bite back a self-satisfied smile, suddenly extremely grateful I've stuck to my gym routine. There won't be any body-building competitions in my future, but judging by Issy's expression, I can keep up with a gorgeous twenty-three-year-old when the occasion calls for it.

"I—" She shakes her head like she's trying to clear it. "I shouldn't."

"It's just a swim," I cajole. "I promise not to fuck you senseless tonight, but just so we're clear"—I unbutton my shorts and kick them away so I'm standing before her wearing only black boxer briefs—"I want to. Very badly."

Her soft, winded noise makes it clear she hasn't missed the effect she's had on me, but still, she doesn't move. "Judah," she pleads, staring at me like I'm betraying her somehow. "You don't understand. I'm not... You don't want me."

I set my glasses aside, the plastic clinking against the metal tabletop. I can't see her as well as I did, and never before have I so regretted not wearing my damn contacts.

"I want you more than I want my next breath, sweetheart. Not just the pieces you've decided are good enough to show the world, but *fucking all of you.*" A sense of calm finality has settled over me. We haven't even kissed. I barely know her, yet I mean these words more than the ones I spoke when I married Reuben's mother all those years ago. It's a promise, and one I intend to honor until this woman stands in front of me in a white dress, ready to make vows of her own.

The best things in my life have come at the end of a long fight; I should have guessed that my future wife would be no exception. I'll fight for her, as long as it takes, until I've stripped away all those perfectly valid reasons she's using to keep me at arm's length.

Isobel Bradley is mine.

"Take your clothes off. Or these are going too." I gesture to my boxer briefs, which do nothing to hide the long, straining ridge of my erection. Apparently, she takes the threat seriously because a moment later, her little summer dress is being tugged over her head and thrown off to join my clothes.

And now it's my turn to stare.

Or try to anyway, until I fumble for my glasses and shove them back on my face. I'm acting like a lunatic, but I'm too far gone to care. I need to see her.

She wasn't wearing a goddamn bra. Fuck me, I wasn't mentally prepared for this. I thought we'd swim, that it would help her sleep and hopefully break down her defenses a little more, but my promise not to sleep with her tonight is starting to feel like complete bullshit. Her breasts are perky, tight, and topped with dusky, pebbled nipples that I want to suck between my teeth. The only thing covering her body is a white cotton thong molded over her cunt.

Issy's chin juts out, and she crosses her arms over her

chest. She's such a proud, fiery little thing for me, and it makes me smug as hell to know that I'm the only one who gets to see this side of her. "You probably do dozens of exams a day. I'm sure you've seen breasts before, *Doctor Hale*."

"Not yours." I see her tremble as I stalk toward her, not stopping until her tight little nipples brush against my chest. We're wrapped up in each other, breathing the same air, and I have to ball my fists at my sides to stop myself from taking it further. I won't touch her until she asks me to. "You're so fucking beautiful, Is. Every inch of you." I let my eyes roam hungrily over her body. "I'm not hiding what you do to me anymore."

The helpless, ragged noise she makes in response sends heat curling up my spine.

"I have a confession to make." My cock is leaking so much precum that there's a dark, wet spot spreading over my boxers. "My bungalow is next door. I saw you the first night we were here, swimming... I've had to jerk myself off three times a day to thoughts of how you looked in that little bikini, Issy. I'm too old for that shit. Let me come in your pussy instead."

"*Judah*," she pleads, looking up at me with this betrayed, pained look. I know it's low, using her physical attraction to me against her, but I have to play every card I have. I'll be so good to her, *she just needs to let me.*

I drop my head, letting my forehead rest against hers. "Let me kiss you, *just* kiss you. Please, Is. Just say yes."

Until the day I die, I'll be grateful I was looking into her eyes at the exact moment she broke. I see it happen, panic turning to acceptance turning to unguarded desire in a fraction of a second. I don't even have time to move first because my girl has thrown herself at me, kissing me so fiercely it makes my chest ache and my already stiff cock throb.

I've had a lot of first kisses in my life, but I know this one will be my last from the moment I get my first taste of her.

I groan, pulling her body against mine as we fucking devour each other. The way her body fits against mine, the way she tastes, the whiny little noises she makes when I grab her perky ass to pull us even closer... Every single thing about this turns me on. The only thing separating us is two flimsy layers of fabric, and it would be so easy to tug her panties aside and thrust into her tight heat. I could have her right here, tuck her back into bed with my cum leaking out of her, and enjoy every second of it.

She isn't in this, though. Not like I am.

It takes every ounce of willpower I have to pull away and press my forehead against hers, both of us panting. "I'm coming for you, Isobel Bradley," I joke quietly, my voice strained from the effort it takes not to kiss her all over again. "You can run, but you can't hide."

FROM: E.BRADLEY@COLUMBIAMED.COM

TO: C.HOLMESBRADLEY@NYCMED.COM, JBRADLEY@NYCMED.COM,
R.HALE@COLUMBIAMED.COM, J.HALE@CDC.GOV,
KENNEDY@LUCASREALTY.COM, NOLAN@LUCAS REALTY.COM,
TOM@LUCASREALTY.COM, I.BRADLEY@UCHICAGO.EDU

SUBJECT: DAY 4: ITINERARY OVERVIEW

Get ready to snorkel, everyone!

8:30 a.m. - Arrive at resort rental shop (located beside entrance to main beach) to pick up your snorkel equipment.
9:00 a.m. - Arrive at the resort harbor to meet our chartered boat, which will take us to the island, where we will be snorkeling.
9:15 a.m. - Departure. Brunch is served on board.
9:45 a.m. - Arrive at Island. An emergency satellite phone and first-aid kit will be on hand, just in case (I think we have the personnel to handle any small issues! lol)
12:30 p.m. - Lunch on beach
4:00 p.m. - Boat returns to take us back to the resort
***Dinner will not be a formal event tonight, though Reuben and I will be eating in the resort cafe if anyone wants to join us!

We hope everybody is excited!

Evie & Reuben

nine

ISOBEL

AS IF THIS "VACATION" hasn't been full of enough unwelcome surprises, the next morning brings yet another complication in the form of Reuben's half-brother, Nolan.

He's a few years older than me and working as a real estate broker for his father's firm. From the moment I step onto the dock where we're meeting the boat taking us on the snorkeling trip, I feel his eyes on me. Kennedy and Mom exchange conspiratorial looks when he greets me a little too warmly, taking the trouble to help me over the small gap between the boat and the dock. There's an empty seat which just so happens to be next to his at the brunch table set up for us on board.

Unluckily for Nolan, Judah is on my other side.

"Not sweet enough, Doc?" I ask him when Nolan offers to refill my mimosa for the third time, and Judah glowers down at his grapefruit like it's personally wronged him. I know I can use this situation to my advantage. If I flirt with Nolan a little, maybe let him think I'm interested, Judah will back off. It would be the best way to put an end to this *thing* once and for all.

It's already gone far enough.

That kiss... Every single thought and reservation was blown straight out of my head the moment I saw the man without his shirt on. I'd been seconds from begging him to take my virginity right there on the back deck, consequences be damned. I lose control around him, and my life has devolved into a shitshow enough as it is. I have no idea how my parents will react when I tell them about Weston, and somehow I don't think it would help matters if they found out I fucked Evie's father-in-law.

I refuse to think about why I can't bring myself to do more than smile politely at Nolan or why I find Judah's jealousy oddly cute.

Very calmly, as though there aren't half a dozen people around us who could notice at any time, Judah reaches out to grip my thigh. I look around wildly, expecting to see shocked eyes on us, but everyone is distracted by Tom's animated story about fishing in Nantucket. Even Nolan has taken his eyes off me for the first time since we sat down and is laughing along with his father's story.

"Don't even think about it," Judah mutters under his breath, running his fingers gently back and forth over the sensitive skin of my inner thigh. He's barely touching me, but I can hardly breathe.

Oh god.

"I don't know what you mean," I lie automatically, keeping my voice as quiet as possible.

"You know exactly what I mean, and it won't work." His fingers move a little higher, and I instinctively part my legs to make more room for him. *What am I doing?* It's like my mind has lost complete control of my body.

His lips twitch, and he takes a long drink of water with his free hand, eyes on the horizon. We're approaching a tiny island surrounded by crystal-blue water, and the only signs of civilization I can see are a long dock and a little area at the end with a few picnic tables set up. Everyone is looking the other way, exclaiming over the beauty of the place, and Judah leans over, his lips brushing against my ear.

"If I see you so much as smile at him again, I'll put you over my knee and spank your ass red. Are we clear?"

I keep my face straight, as though I hadn't heard him, as Judah straightens up and returns to his grapefruit, leaving his hand on my thigh beneath the table.

When Nolan turns back to face me, grinning, I don't return his smile.

* * *

It doesn't take long for me to get sick of snorkeling.

I love the water, and the fish are beautiful. Still, I wouldn't call it fun when I'm accompanied at all times by a flirty realtor and Judah, who clearly doesn't want to give me a chance to work up the nerve to employ the diversionary tactic I was considering on the boat.

After a quarter of an hour, when Nolan touches my arm to draw my attention to some coral and Judah "accidentally" smacks him in the face with his flipper, I'm done. I wave to both of them and swim off toward the beach, ripping off my flippers and goggles as soon as the water is deep enough to stand up in and stomp out of the waves like the world's grumpiest mermaid.

In my first stroke of good luck since I got off the plane, the beach is empty, and I'm afforded a few moments of peace as I walk over the hot sand to the table where I left my bag.

If I have to endure one more minute of Judah's jealousy,

Nolan's flirting, or my mother's and Kennedy's completely transparent attempts to shove the two of us together, I'm going to burst. It's too much, too many feelings, too many people. I'm emotionally drained from my panic attack yesterday, my sister's father-in-law telling me he wants to come inside me, and trying to figure out how to tell my parents I didn't get into Weston.

It's not like that's my only option. I have acceptances from three other medical schools I applied to as backups. If I want to become a doctor, I still can. I hate to admit it, but Judah's words have gotten under my skin. He asked me questions I've never dared ask myself, ones that the denial letter is now forcing me to confront.

Do I want this? Do I *really* want this?

No.

I've asked myself that question over and over again today and keep coming up with the same answer. If nobody else factored into this decision but me... *No*. I wouldn't go. Everything about being a doctor sounds terrifying to me. I don't love it. I'm not even particularly interested in it. I have to figure out what I want, but what else am I supposed to do? Who do I want to be, if not another Doctor Bradley?

I love working with the kids at the daycare, but could I do that every day?

"Issy." My hands pause, buried in my bag in search of sunscreen, as I hear the sounds of soft footsteps over the sand.

Judah.

"Go away. I need a minute." I don't bother to look back at him. "*And don't call me that*," I add as an afterthought.

I find the bottle of lotion and pour some into my hand, rubbing it furiously over my chest and shoulders. I know he hasn't left, but I don't acknowledge him, waiting for him to give me something else to snarl at him over.

"Let me help." I didn't realize he's moved closer to me, and I suck in a surprised breath when a large hand comes around my side to pluck the bottle from my hands.

I'd like to turn and argue with him, but I know what he looks like in those blue swim trunks, and keeping my eyes turned safely away toward the ocean seems safer. The little picnic area is out of sight of the area where everyone is snorkeling, hidden by a thicket of palm trees and brush, but someone could still come walking around the corner at any moment. Just like when he put his hand on my thigh at breakfast, though, getting caught doesn't seem to worry Judah.

"You'd have a hard time explaining this," I tell him coldly as the bottle shuts with a click. A moment later, Judah's hands meet my back, smoothing sunscreen over my body. I can barely breathe as he takes his time rubbing it into my skin, hands never moving lower than the top of my bikini bottom.

Judah hums thoughtfully, and when he speaks, I can hear a smile in his voice. "I'm a physician, Issy. I'm morally obligated to protect you from skin cancer."

"This isn't funny. Aren't you worried about people knowing?"

"Knowing what?"

His hands move to my right arm, and I clear my throat, tearing my eyes away from the sight of his fingers slowly massaging my skin to stare at the bottom of the closest palm tree. "Knowing that you're, you know..." I trail off lamely, my cheeks burning from frustration and arousal. Why does he have to make me feel so good? This would all be so much easier if I didn't get wet just seeing the man's face.

"That I'm panting after a gorgeous little cocktease half my age?" he suggests mildly, and I have to bite my tongue to keep myself from whimpering. His hands leave my arm for a moment, and I hear the sunscreen bottle being opened and closed again before they move back to my left arm. "This isn't something I do, just so you know," he offers, suddenly sounding a little worried. "I haven't dated anyone in years, and certainly not a woman your age. I didn't want you to think—"

"That you're into me because I'm a gorgeous little cocktease half your age?"

He chuckles. "Yes. Because no, that's not why I'm *into you*, Issy." I want to ask why he *is* because I genuinely don't know, but I keep my mouth shut. Giving him any additional opportunities to charm my panties off is the opposite of what I should be doing. "To answer your question, no, I don't particularly care. I'd rather it not come out before Reuben and Evie's wedding to spare them the drama, but I won't keep my hands off you to spare feelings."

He's talking like we're in a relationship, and we're not. We're just... I don't know what this is, but whatever worries I have about what the hell I'm doing evaporate when Judah's hands move to my hips, running his fingers over my pelvic bones. I whimper, slapping a hand over my mouth a second later. If Judah heard, he gives no indication of it, and I'm a little relieved he's not saying more of what he did last night because I'd probably spontaneously combust. He has me so worked up, so frustrated and desperate. I went for a four-mile run this morning before breakfast, and it didn't help one bit.

"Have you done your legs yet?"

I shake my head mutely, heart pounding wildly in my chest.

His hands start low, smoothing the lotion slowly over my ankles and up my calves. There's no way in hell I can explain this, even to myself. *I was going to avoid him.* Not only am I not walking away, I'm asking for more. My breathing turns ragged when Judah's hands slip between my thighs, rubbing the lotion into the sensitive skin.

I'm so wet it's embarrassing. If he even brushes his hand against my swimsuit, I'm positive he'll be able to tell.

"Do you need more?" he murmurs, and I almost collapse when I find the courage to look back at the gorgeous man kneeling in the sand behind me, his silver hair damp from the ocean and erection tenting his swim trunks. His hands stop on my hips, holding me in place, and I know he isn't asking if I need more lotion.

I want to say yes, but I'm scared. What if the way he makes me feel is a fluke, and I really am as messed up as I've always thought? I've embarrassed myself enough around him. If he touches me more, he's going to enter the next level in humiliating Isobel Bradley trivia.

"Issy," Judah whispers my name like a prayer, and the scales finally tilt.

I want to cry when I finally nod, fear and hope twisting inside me. "Yes."

His head falls forward with a deep groan of relief, pressing against my lower back as he moves a hand to cup my entire sex through my swimsuit. My hips cant forward immediately, a throaty cry coming from between my parted lips. Just the pressure of his touch feels incredible, and I can't help grinding shamelessly down, pleasure knotting low in my tummy.

"Do you need me to put my fingers inside you?" Judah

coos, giving my pussy a little squeeze through the material. Apparently, my little moan is an acceptable answer because a moment later, he's hooked my swimsuit to the side, baring my slippery, swollen pussy to his gaze. "*Fuck*, Issy. Is all this for me? Do I make you wet, sweetheart?"

"Yes." I hiccup, fruitlessly trying to grind myself back on him, but this position won't allow it. He knows what I need, though, because he slides two fingers forward, circling my clit gently. It's impossibly erotic, and I think I might die if he stops. I've never felt anything like this, never even come close during all those nights alone in my bed, rubbing my clit frantically in an attempt to relieve the tension built up inside me. Already my whole body is shaking, and it feels like my entire awareness is centered on the gentle swipes of Judah's fingers.

Oh my god. I want him to touch me more. I want his fingers inside me, spreading me open, *breaking me*. I want to stand here in the middle of a beach with our family members in the ocean only a few hundred yards away, my legs spread wide for my sister's future father-in-law. I want his big, strong body behind me, his hands holding me steady as he eases his cock into my throbbing sex.

"Bend over for me. Hold onto the table, that's it." His voice is so calm, but there's a low strain to it I've never heard before. He drags my legs further apart, and a second later, he's leaned forward, and his fingers are replaced with his tongue.

Holy hell.

My arms almost give out and send me face-first into the picnic table when he pushes his tongue into my throbbing opening, groaning like *he* is having the time of his life..

All I can do is hold onto the edge of the picnic table, my

muscles shaking and my breath coming in desperate, fevered pants.

I've had ex-boyfriends do this to me before, or at least something that bears a passing resemblance to this. This has all the same major elements—my legs spread, a man with his face buried between them, tonguing my opening and my clit—but there's one major difference here. I'm enjoying this... A lot. Not only does it feel good, it feels like my body is hurtling toward something. A hook is being pulled from low in my belly, dragging me closer and closer to an edge I've never even seen before.

Is it possible he's actually going to make me have an orgasm? Is that what's happening to me?

If so... the hype is real.

"Judah." I hear myself crying over and over again, far too loud. Somebody could hear, somebody could *see us*. My family, *his family*, are in the water, only a few hundred yards away. I've needed this for so long, though, and as Judah's stubble brushes against my inner thighs and his fingers bite painfully into my hips to hold me still, I'm almost hysterical with the need to finish.

"Fuck, yes." He growls when he pulls back. That's all the warning I get before his long, thick fingers plunge roughly into my opening, making me yelp in surprise and pain as something inside me tears.

Shit.

Behind me, Judah has frozen. I can barely breathe as he slowly pulls his fingers free. Peeking over my shoulder, my heart plummets when I see him staring down at his hand, which has two fingers smeared with fresh, bright-red blood. I open my mouth to say something, make some excuse that doesn't exist to blow it off like it's no big deal, but I hear something else first.

Voices from further down the beach are coming closer.

We barely have time to straighten up, me tugging my bikini bottoms back into place while Judah adjusts his erection before my father and Tom turn the corner, snorkeling gear in hand.

For a second, I think it's all over. Surely they'll be able to see what just happened written all over my face, because how am I supposed to be unaffected by this?

"Judah! Shit, did you cut yourself?" Dad asks loudly. He frowns in concern, looking at the smear of blood on Judah's long fingers, which he didn't have time to wipe away.

I turn away, unable to hide my horrified look and snatch the sunscreen off the ground just for something to do.

"It's nothing. I already stopped bleeding," I hear Judah reply calmly, waving Dad off when he starts to move closer. Out of the corner of my eye, I see him wipe the blood off on his towel.

"Isobel, I think Nolan was looking for you." Tom chuckles as he unscrews the top of his water bottle. "I apologize in advance if he's pushy. The kid was practically raised by real estate agents. He's not very familiar with *subtle*."

I don't look at Judah as I edge around the picnic table, overly conscious of the sharp ache between my legs. "It's fine," I say, but my throat tightens when I realize Dad is looking at me. He's *really* looking at me, and there's dark suspicion in his eyes.

ten

ISOBEL

THE SUN IS low in the sky by the time everyone has
had enough of snorkeling, and we climb back on the boat,
tired and tan.

I can still feel the ache that Judah's fingers left inside
me. Every time I see him lift his bottle of water to his lips or
adjust his glasses, I press my thighs together as my sex
gives a dull throb. I can't look at him without blushing, but
it gets so much worse when we get off the boat back at the
resort and my mother's hand reaches out to snatch my
wrist as I pass.

"What have you done to yourself, Isobel?"

I never bothered to get completely redressed, just threw
on a cropped t-shirt, and you can clearly see most of my
lower half. Mom's eyes are narrowed, and she's glaring
down at my hip, where there are five small, round bruises.
For a moment, I'm confused, racking my brain for how I
possibly could have gotten them, but when I glance down
at my other side and see more, my body floods with heat
when I realize what they are.

Fingerprints. From Judah's hands squeezing my hips when he bent me over and ate my pussy like his last meal.

I open my mouth, trying to think of any reasonable excuse for how this could have happened, but nothing comes out. I allow her to pull me around, watching her face get rigid when she sees the matching set. She doesn't know *who*—I hope—but it's pretty obvious *what*. If Dad even mentions he saw Judah and me alone on the beach....

"No idea," I lie, pulling away from her to scramble back onto the dock, feeling the weight of everyone's eyes on me. Great, just *great*. I'm a virgin, and the entire family is still going to think I've been sleeping around. Or wait, *am I* still a virgin? Do fingers count?

I quickly decide, no. They don't. Especially in comparison to the monster dick I've seen threatening to rip out of Judah's pants. When we—

I'm halfway down the dock when my steps falter, and my mouth suddenly feels dry. *When* I have sex with Judah? Since when is fucking Evie's father-in-law a foregone conclusion? Glancing over my shoulder, I see him watching me closely, oblivious to my father's attempts to make conversation with him.

I need to get out of here. My heart pounds against my ribcage as I hurry down the path leading to the main resort area, pretending not to notice him following me. Energy is strung tightly between us, vibrating in the darkening night air and practically humming the closer we get to our bungalows. I don't once turn to look at or acknowledge him, but when I finally fumble with my keycard and burst into the darkened bungalow, I don't bother closing the door behind me.

I don't have to wait long. The door thuds closed a

moment later, and I stare down at my hands, gripping the back of the nearest armchair.

This feels so surreal, so incredibly impossible that I'm feeling all these things. It's overwhelming, wonderful, and terrifying all at once, and when I finally find the courage to turn to face Judah, my eyes are full of tears. He's already seen me at some of my weakest moments and knows things I can barely acknowledge to myself. When does it all become too much? I've spent twenty-three years putting up walls that this man has managed to demolish in three days. He sees me, all of me, and if he decides to walk away after I give him this last piece of myself, I'm sure I'll never recover.

"I had a mental breakdown." His expression flickers, but he doesn't say a word, just stares at me from his place beside the front door as I talk. "It's why I'm graduating a year late. It's why my parents are so weird with me. Well, partially why." I shake my head, tears streaming down my cheeks. "I was having panic attack after panic attack. I tried so many different medications, and nothing worked. I ended up losing it in the middle of a final exam. You don't want to get involved with me. I'm... I'm a mess. Please just go. *Please.*"

Please don't go.

He doesn't move, but when he speaks, his voice is a low drawl. "Is that supposed to scare me off, Is?"

"I've never had an orgasm," I spit in desperation. "I've tried. I'm broken, Judah. I'm fucked up. Go. Leave."

Outside, the forecasted rain seems to have finally arrived. Thunder rumbles in the distance, and fat drops of rain sound muffled on the thatched roof. Still, Judah doesn't move. "You think there's something wrong with you?" he asks quietly, his lips pulling back into a snarl like I've said something foul.

"I *know* there is,' I retort, folding my arms over my chest, trying in vain to keep myself together.

Judah's jaw clenches, and he takes a step toward me. I can barely breathe as he closes the distance between us and looms over me, his eyes bright and intense. "Listen to me.'" He grips my jaw, forcing me to meet his gaze when I try to turn away. "You're not broken, sweetheart. You're a fucking *miracle*, and I'm going to prove it over and over again until you believe me. Starting now."

Without warning, he leans forward and grabs the backs of my legs, throwing me over his shoulder like I weigh nothing.

"What—" I squeal, fisting the back of his t-shirt to keep myself from falling, but I don't need to. Judah's arm is wrapped around my legs, keeping me in place as he marches through the bungalow. I know where he's going, but my stomach swoops when he leans over and deposits me on the big, fluffy white bed. Outside, rain is starting to fall heavily. Wrapped in the noise of it and the semi-darkness, I'm *really* having a hard time remembering all the reasons I'm not supposed to want this man.

"You know what I do for a living, don't you, Issy?"

I blink up at him, confused and more than a little turned on by the way he's looking at my body. "Um, you're a doctor?"

His lips curl into a dangerous, smug smile. "You happen to be in a room with one of the most respected Obstetricians and Gynecologists in the country, Miss Bradley." I gasp as his hands grip my ankles, and he drags me to the edge of the bed. "Now, you said you were having difficulty reaching orgasm?"

My brain has short-circuited, and my body has taken

over. That's the only possible explanation for why I find myself nodding breathlessly, heart in my throat.

"Let's take a look." His fingers catch the band of my bikini bottoms, and he pulls them down my legs. A low rumble of approval sounds from deep in his chest as he brings them right to his nose and inhales greedily.

"Judah," I squeak, squirming when he tosses them away and turns his gaze to my aching sex. I'm positive he can see how wet I am. I took the time to get a bikini wax before coming here, knowing how much time I'd spend in a bathing suit, and my smooth skin is glistening with the arousal I've already made for him.

He smirks, straightening for a moment to roll up the sleeves of his pullover, exposing toned forearms dusted with dark hair. "Put your heels right here at the edge of the bed, Miss Bradley. That's it." His warm hands guide my thighs apart so I'm completely open and exposed to him.

His tone is so professional and detached, it's like we really are in a doctor's office. Like he's my physician and this examination is going to be purely clinical. We're not, though. I'm spread out, nearly naked, at the edge of a massive white bed, and my sister's future father-in-law is giving me a dirty doctor exam.

Holy hell.

"Yes," I confess finally, my belly knotting as I feel two fingers slide between the lips of my pussy and spread them gently open.

"And is this during masturbation or with partners?" On the last word, his tone drops and becomes darker, more threatening.

I'm practically shaking now, and I force my eyes open to find Judah looking right at me. "By myself," I admit, my chest heaving and my cheeks burning. "I've never—I mean, a few guys tried, but nothing happened."

He already knows I'm a virgin; he popped my cherry on his fingers only a few hours ago, but his eyes still flash with triumph as he nods. "Very smart." He's a doctor. He probably sees about a thousand vaginas a year, but I'm pretty positive he doesn't look at them like this, or there would be a line of horny patients outside his practice every morning. "I'm going to apply some stimulation, Miss Bradley. To test your... responsiveness."

My whole body jolts as he leans forward, his hot tongue meeting my aching sex. I gasp, bucking and squirming as he licks me decadently from my clenching core up to circle my clit. He sucks it between his lips, his free hand pressing my hips down as they shoot off the bed.

Oh my god. This feels... like nothing I've ever felt before. I'm almost drunk on the pleasure, and I grip his hair greedily, trying to keep him there. How does he know exactly what I need?

I could cry when he pulls back.

"Judah."

His eyes flash dangerously from beneath his ruffled hair and glasses sitting askew on his nose. "You seem exceptionally responsive and sensitive to me, Miss Bradley. Is that normal for you?"

I shake my head, wishing he would go back to sucking my clit. I'm even more worked up and frustrated than I was when we got off the boat.

Like he knows what I'm thinking, Judah smirks. Drawing his fingers down, he circles my entrance slowly, applying more pressure on each pass until his fingers have slipped inside me, and he's fucking me gently with them. "Do you feel any pain?"

There's something so erotic about the slow, measured way he's touching me. It does hurt, and I'm still sore from earlier, but the pain somehow makes the pleasure more intense. He's actually going to make me come. This is happening. I reach up to grip my own breasts, twisting my nipples roughly. "It hurts so good. Oh god, *Judah*—"

"Do you know what I think?" He growls, plunging back into me with a third finger, making me squeal and open my legs wider, instinctively trying to make room for him. "I think you're going to be spreading your legs for me morning, noon, and night, begging for this. How would that make those little shits who tried this before me feel? Knowing an old man gets to enjoy what a desperate, horny little thing you are? To know I'm the only one who makes you come? *Fuck*, you're so wet for me. This pussy is going to feel so tight when it's wrapped around my fat dick."

My whole body is strung tight, my loud cries filling the room with every stroke of his expert fingers. I'm so close, can feel myself approaching an edge I didn't even know existed.

Judah growls, fucking me harder. "That's it. Take it, sweetheart. You're close, aren't you? Going to have your first orgasm on my fingers?"

He leans forward and sucks my clit between his teeth, flicking it rapidly with his tongue.

And then it happens.

I explode. My back bows off the bed, and I shudder, letting out a feeble, hoarse cry as pleasure rushes over me, surging from my scalp to the tips of my toes. It seems to go on and on, but Judah doesn't move. He keeps gently sucking my clit until I've collapsed back to the mattress, and the fingers I wound in his hair are trying to pull him away.

"You made me come," I mumble hazily, watching as he wipes his face with the back of his hand and crawls over my body to kiss me deeply. I can taste myself on his tongue.

"I sure did." He chuckles smugly when we break apart, leaning forward to nip at the delicate skin below my ear. "I'm going to do it again too. As many times as you want."

I feel so good, relaxed and happy, and *hopeful*. I'm out of control, completely disconnected from the person I've been trying to be for so long, and it's exhilarating.

Judah shifts his weight to the side of me, and I follow, pushing him over flat on his back. His eyes widen with surprise as I lean forward to kiss him again, one of my hands reaching down to stroke his cock through the swim trunks he's still wearing. I want to reduce him to the same shuddering, oversensitive mess he's made of me.

"You seem exceptionally responsive and sensitive to me, Doctor Hale. Is that normal for you?" I ask coyly, throwing his words back at him as I slip my hand beneath his shorts, wrapping my hand around him for the first time.

Holy shit, he's big.

Judah's chest quakes in a quiet laugh, which turns to a groan when I squeeze him tighter. "No, Miss Bradley, it's not."

Biting back a grin, I lean over to kiss his neck, scraping my teeth gently over a spot that makes him hiss and buck into my hand. I've spent all this time consumed by his effect on me. Somehow, it never occurred to me that this wild connection could go both ways. I never thought about how *good* that would feel.

I move slowly, crawling down his body, unzipping his pullover and lifting his t-shirt to kiss the trail of dark hair below his belly button. He's already panting when I tug on the waistband of his shorts and curses quietly as he lifts his hips to let me get rid of them. I feel powerful and wanted. So, so wanted.

"Do you want me to put my mouth on it?" I ask innocently, stroking his shaft gently up and down, enough to tease him but not enough to bring him any closer to finishing.

Judah groans, his hands fisting the sheets as I lean forward to run my tongue along the bottom of his cock, feeling myself growing wet all over again. "Don't play with me, little girl. I'm in no fucking state to handle it."

In response, I lean forward and wrap my lips around the head of his cock, slowly circling it with my tongue. Salty pre-cum begins to flow steadily for me as I bob my head up and down, licking him the best I can around his intimidating thickness.

I once heard my freshman-year roommate talking to her friends about a guy she'd hooked up with, complaining that "there's such a thing as too big" and that her cervix was probably bruised. I'd been embarrassed and confused about why I found that so hot, but now that I've found a real-life monster cock of my own, I get it. Just the thought of Judah's big hands holding my legs open, his face full of the pleasure he's feverishly taking from my body, is enough to make me moan around his length and bob my head lower.

He likes it. I can tell by the way the muscles of his thighs tense and how his balls draw up tight to his body.

"Fuck, yes." Judah groans from above me, his hands tangling in my hair to control the speed and depth of my movements. "Don't you dare spit, do you hear me? Keep it on your tongue, and let me see how gorgeous you look with a mouth full of my cum."

I choke slightly when the fat head of his dick hits the

back of my throat, but Judah doesn't relent. A few breath-less, desperate seconds later, he stills, finishing with a long groan as his seed spills over my tongue in thick spurts. When his hands relax slightly, I pull back to look at him and open my mouth wide, obediently showing him just like he asked.

Judah hisses, his chest heaving. "*Fuck.* Good girl."

He doesn't leave. I'm not sure why I expected he might, but I'm still surprised when Judah pulls me back onto the bed and curls his naked body around mine. His cock goes from soft to hard again quickly, but apart from nestling it against my ass, he does nothing to move us toward round two.

He holds me until his breathing turns long and even.

The panic sets in soon after that.

FROM:	E.BRADLEY@COLUMBIAMED.COM
TO:	C.HOLMESBRADLEY@NYCMED.COM, JBRADLEY@NYCMED.COM, R.HALE@COLUMBIAMED.COM, J.HALE@CDC.GOV, KENNEDY@LUCASREALTY.COM, NOLAN@LUCAS REALTY.COM, TOM@LUCASREALTY.COM, I.BRADLEY@UCHICAGO.EDU

SUBJECT: DAY 5: ITINERARY OVERVIEW

Time to Party!!!

You'll notice a lot more familiar faces wandering around the resort as friends and family begin to arrive for the wedding. Unfortunately, that means the family-only events have ended for the weekend, but we're so excited to celebrate with all of you!

Kennedy, Caroline, Isobel, Reuben, and myself will be spending most of the day getting things in order for the rehearsal dinner tomorrow.

Nolan & Isobel - The bachelor/bachelorette party begins at 8 p.m.

Tom, John & Judah - The lounge has reserved a table for you at 8 p.m.

Kennedy & Caroline - The spa got back to me and apparently, they do not offer anti-aging treatments on site. I booked you both in for hot stone massages beginning at 7:30 p.m.

Evie & Reuben

eleven

JUDAH

I CAN'T THINK of anything I would rather do less than have drinks with Tom and John.

A root canal would at least be productive.

Most of Evie's and Reuben's friends have arrived for the combined bachelor and bachelorette party tonight, so the resort is suddenly full of young doctors. It's irrational, but I don't want to let Isobel out of my sight. Last night was a breakthrough. She opened up to me in a real way, and she was willingly vulnerable. If the previous few days have taught me anything, however, I knew that she would try to pull away. I was ready for it, but it was still like a punch to the gut when I woke up this morning to find the bed beside me cold and empty.

I haven't seen her all day. Now, she'll be in the resort's nightclub with fucking *Nolan* and a pack of my son's friends, all of who are single, age-appropriate doctors, whom her parents would thoroughly approve of. Meanwhile, I'm sitting in the lounge having drinks and smoking cigars with her prick father and my ex-wife's husband.

"There he is," Tom booms over the dimly lit lounge

when I walk inside, irritated and practically crawling out of my skin with the need to pull Issy into a dark corner and make sure she remembers who makes her feel.

Tom and John already have drinks and are leaning back in a pair of club chairs, cigars between their fingers. As I sit down, John throws back the rest of his scotch with a satisfied hiss. "Let me buy you both a glass of this. It's excellent," he offers, leaning over to signal the bartender. "Where have you been all day, Hale?"

Wandering the resort in search of your daughter, mostly.

"Just had to take care of some work." I drum my fingers on the arm of the chair. How long do I have to sit here making small talk with the man I've grown to despise?

John is oblivious to my preoccupation. "All work, no play? Still? The other residents *hated* him," he tells Tom, chortling. "He never left the hospital. Made them all look slackers by comparison."

Everything that comes out of this man's mouth puts my teeth on edge.

Tom makes an offhand observation about my work ethic, and I lose track of the conversation. Instead, I find myself staring out the nearest window, which has a view of the pathway leading toward the resort's nightclub. I can't stop thinking about last night, the sexy, shocked look on her face when I gave her that first orgasm, and how good it felt to fall asleep with her in my arms. One night wasn't enough. It wasn't *close* to enough. My previous fixation with Isobel has bloomed into a full-blown obsession, and it's terrifying.

She wants me, that much is clear, but I'm not discounting the possibility she could still run from this. We only have so much time left at the resort—

"Judah?"

I blink, looking back over at John and Tom, who are staring at me, bemused. "Sorry." I shake my head and shoot them a strained smile. "What were you saying?"

Tom nods toward the tumbler resting on the table before me. "Your drink is here. Thinking about the wedding?"

"Yes," I lie, picking it up and taking a long sip that burns my throat on the way down but does, at least, take the edge off.

John nods knowingly. "I feel the same way. Can't believe how fast it all went. She's always been such a brilliant young woman, and I won't pretend I'm not excited to see how the next few years pan out. What steps she'll take."

"And Isobel too, I'm sure." Tom smiles, lifting his glass in a silent toast. "You and Caroline raised two great young women. Nolan certainly seems taken with your youngest. Maybe we'll have another wedding to celebrate. Crazier things have happened."

Crazier things *have* happened, but this one sure as fuck won't.

"Of course," John replies without any real enthusiasm, swirling his drink. "It should be interesting to see what Weston makes of her."

What the hell does that mean?

Tom frowns like he doesn't quite get it, either. "Isobel's quite the student as well, isn't she? Evie told us she's a very hard worker as well. She speaks very highly of her sister."

John sighs, looking put upon. "Isobel isn't unintelligent. I hate to say it, but I don't think she'll do well there even if she does manage to get in. She doesn't quite *have it*, if you know what I mean. It isn't a matter of working hard or even making it through med school. It's *raw talent* and the ability to handle your shit when it hits the fan. Isobel doesn't have that."

The sounds of the lounge have died away, and suddenly all I can hear is a sharp ringing while John's mouth keeps moving, callously listing off all the qualities about his daughter, the woman I love, that don't quite meet his standards.

This motherfucker.

Whatever restraint I've been employing for Reuben's sake is nowhere to be found. Before I can stop myself, I'm on my feet. John's expression barely has time to register shock before I'm looming over him in his chair, my hand gripping the collar of his shirt so hard he chokes.

"Listen to me, you pompous asshole," I hiss, staring directly into his watering eyes, ignoring Tom's alarmed yell and the sounds of commotion around us. "The way you and Caroline treat Isobel is disgusting. You treat *her* like she isn't good enough? As if your Daddy didn't need to buy your ass into Weston, and the whole goddamn medical community doesn't know about that malpractice lawsuit you settled last year. You're a fraud, coasting by on a famous last name, and if you don't learn to keep your *fucking* mouth shut, I'll put my fist in it next time. Do I make myself clear?"

John sucks in an unsteady breath. Without waiting for an answer, I shove him back into his chair and stalk out through the silent, staring lounge.

I fucked up. I let my temper get the better of me, and I know he isn't going to let this go. The man is fueled by pride and ego. Me publicly shaming and insulting him won't go over well. I personally don't give a shit what John Bradley thinks of me or, more likely, runs his mouth about me. I *do*, however, give a shit about my son being able to marry the woman he loves without stress and Issy not being plunged further into family turmoil.

I'm still so pissed off that I'm barely conscious of walking back to my bungalow until I'm standing in front of the door with a hollow ache in my chest. I want to see her, feel her body against mine, and now I won't until tomorrow at the rehearsal dinner. Everything feels like it's unraveling, and there's not a thing I can do about it. The next few days will be chaotic—I'll be lucky to get a moment alone with Isobel—and then we'll be off to separate corners of the country. *I need more time.*

Knowing there's nothing I can do about it tonight, I push open the bungalow door. I expected the inside to be dark and quiet as I left it, but it's not. The bedroom light is on, and the gaping hole in my chest seems to fill back in when I realize the sound of the shower running.

It couldn't be.

Heart pounding, I pad into the bathroom, stopping short at the unmistakable sight of Isobel's naked silhouette standing behind the foggy glass, her head tilted back into the spray of water.

She came back.

This was the last thing I expected, but I should have known that Isobel Bradley would surprise me. Everything about this woman has been completely unexpected in the very best way, and I'm so goddamn blown away by her that I can barely breathe.

I can't deny it to myself anymore, not after this.

I'm falling in love with her.

I undress quietly and pull open the glass door, my whole soul warming at the sight of her naked and waiting for me. "Hi," she murmurs, watching as I close the door and step beneath the spray of water with her. She looks so gorgeous with water streaming over her bare skin, pink from the heat. I can't say I've ever gone from exhausted and defeated to ecstatic and horny so quickly before.

I reach out to hold her waist, wanting to touch some part of her. "I wasn't expecting you."

"Is it okay that I'm here?" she asks, her expression suddenly worried as if I'm about to take back all the shit I've said over the last few days because I came home to find her naked.

I kiss her slowly, loving how the way she tastes is already so familiar. She leans into me, her hands resting over my bare chest. "Yes, it's okay. More than okay." I chuckle when we break apart. "I thought you were avoiding me."

Isobel's shoulder lifts in a halfhearted shrug. "I was."

"What changed?"

She smiles softly, her eyes searching my face. "I missed you more than I was scared, I guess."

I kiss her again, and I've never felt this full. Everything I've ever wanted is in my arms, holding me just as desperately as I'm holding her. This woman will be my wife, my family, my whole fucking world, and I'm going to make it my life's work to make damn sure she never doubts how much she means to me.

It doesn't take long for our kiss to turn from sweet to heated, my tongue darting out to stroke hers, swallowing her moans as she grinds her naked body against mine. We don't need to talk about this. I know what she needs, and I can't hold back anymore. She wasn't ready for this before, but she is now.

Reaching blindly behind her to turn off the water, we stumble backward out of the shower, kissing frantically. There's not a single part of her that doesn't turn me on, and as much as I want to spend the entire night worshiping every inch of her body, my girl has waited long enough.

We manage to find our way to my bed, and Issy breaks away from me, panting, to crawl back into the center of the mattress. Every time I jerk myself off for the rest of my life, I'm going to think about this moment. My girl. My beautiful, sexy-as-hell girl leaning back on my bed with her little tits heaving and thighs spread as wide as they'll go, silently offering me her untouched pussy.

"Do you want me to fuck you, sweetheart?" I coo, crawling forward until I'm hovering over her, my throbbing cock tracing pre-cum over her stomach.

"Yes." She moans, hooking her legs behind my back. "Do you have a condom?"

I grit my teeth. I don't. Sex with a gorgeous twenty-three-year-old wasn't exactly on the itinerary for this trip, but even if I had a full box on the bedside table, it wouldn't fucking matter. I haven't had unprotected sex since Reuben was conceived. I never wanted to risk it, but with Isobel... I don't want anything between us.

I have to drag my gaze away from her pretty pussy to meet her eyes. "We don't need condoms."

Frustrated, she whines, "Judah, I'm not on birth control."

My cock throbs at her words, but I somehow keep my expression composed. "When did your last menstrual cycle end?"

Her cheeks turn pink, and her mouth pops open in shock, adorable and outraged. *Oh my god.* I'm not your patient, Judah!"

"Thank fuck for that." I guide the head of my cock down, settling myself against her entrance with enough pressure to make her pant and moan, but not enough to actually penetrate her. "Answer the question, Issy."

She huffs. "It ended the day after we got here, but I don't see why it—"

Fuck, I'm messed up for being disappointed by that. "I won't get you pregnant today." I roll my hips forward just a little, teasing her. "You're still outside your fertility window, and I'm clean if that's what you're worried about."

There's a moment when I think she's going to say no. I'm prepared for it, already mentally running through a dozen other ways I can make her come, but I won't need them. Issy's hands smooth over my chest to twine around the back of my neck, and breathlessly, she nods.

It feels like all the air has gone out of me. I've never wanted like I want her. I didn't even know it was possible for my whole body to burn like this, to feel like I might die if I don't get inside her. I'm going to remember this, though, and when I do, I want to remember my girl using my cock to give herself an orgasm for the very first time. I want her to prove to herself how perfect and unbroken she is.

I roll us, and Issy squeaks, her hands splaying over my chest as she finds herself sitting astride me, her wet slit pressed tight to my shaft. "Ride me, sweetheart. Use my fat dick," I beg, squeezing her hips. "Make yourself come."

I'm not the only one who needs this. No sooner have the words left my mouth, Issy is up on her knees, one hand finding my cock and guiding it to her entrance.

"You're really big." She bites her lip, suddenly nervous. "What if it hurts?"

"It will," I tell her honestly, reaching down to rub her clit. I should finger her, help get her ready to take me, but I'm *right there*. "You're going to feel pressure, your muscles are going to burn, but I promise you'll like it."

I expect her to take it slowly, to play with me a little bit and ease herself into it, but as usual, my girl takes me by surprise. She presses down, eyes widening as the fat head of my dick slips inside her, and she gets her first taste of the cock she's going to be taking for the rest of her life. It's the sexiest thing I've ever seen—watching the surprise, how her eyebrows knit together as the pain sets in, and the fear when she begins to wonder if I'm too big for her.

Her fingers dig into my chest. "Ow. Oh god." Her head shakes back and forth frantically, but she still doesn't move off of me. "You're too big. I can't—"

"Look at us," I order her, moving my fingers from her clit so she has a clear view of how her pussy looks stretched snugly around the straining length of my cock, still only halfway inside her. "You're doing so well. Ride me just like this for a little while. It'll get easier when you're stretched out."

She wiggles a little experimentally, and I groan, gritting my teeth to keep myself from thrusting up and giving her more than she's ready for. I'm determined to let her take the lead on this, but that doesn't mean I can't teach her a few things along the way. "Like this." I hold her hips, showing her how to ride me. It's erotic, watching my girl's eyes flutter shut and her lips part with pleasure when she finally finds a rhythm that works for her.

It doesn't take long until she's sliding further down my shaft with each roll of her cute little ass. "Rub your clit," I order, my voice strained with the effort it's taking me to hold back. "Use my dick. Take what you need. You're doing it, baby. Such a good girl for me, taking all that in your virgin cunt."

"I'm gonna come," she slurs, bouncing up and down on my cock, tits bouncing and fingers flying over her clit. I'm so goddamn proud of her when her thighs begin to tremble, and she shoves herself down, taking my entire cock in her tight cunt as she comes with a cry.

It drives me a little insane to know she's been out there in the world all this time, so convinced she's broken. "You're perfect." I groan, rolling us over so she's sprawled on the bed beneath me, legs spread wide open and her eyes still unfocused from the force of the orgasm she gave herself. I slowly pull back and drive back into her roughly, making her suck in a sharp breath. I'm going even deeper like this, and even though I want to keep going more than I want my next breath, I pause. "Eyes on me," I order hoarsely, pulsing my hips slowly instead.

"Judah," Issy whines, but does as she's told, gazing up at me from beneath her long lashes.

God, the things I want to do to her. "I want to fuck you rough. It might hurt." It's the last shred of decency left in me, and Issy rips it to shreds when she moans in response, more wetness flooding over my shaft.

"I want it," she begs in a breathy little voice that makes my cock twitch. "Fuck me rough, Daddy." As the word leaves her mouth, her eyes widen, filling with embarrassment and panic. "I mean—"

"Shhh." I silence her with a kiss, nipping at her full bottom lip. I can't believe anyone could be as lucky as I am now. "Does that turn you on, baby? Do you need Daddy to give it to you nice and hard?"

Issy moans, her cunt tightening around my cock. I feel like it's my first time too, because nothing has ever felt this good. Slowly, determined to satisfy my girl, I pull back and drive into her so hard that the headboard bangs against the wall, and Issy's eyes go wide. Yeah, she likes it like that. So do I.

"Say it again," I plead, reaching down to grip her leg and lift it higher over my hip, fucking her wildly now. Heat is gathering at the base of my spine, and my balls have drawn up tight to my body. I'm so close that I have to bite the inside of my cheek to keep myself from spilling inside her, but it's worth it when Issy's fingers tighten in my hair, and her walls flutter over my length.

"*Daddy*—"

"Oh, fuck."

We come together, her cunt clamping down on me so hard I couldn't have pulled out if I tried. She's everything, *this* is everything, and the moment the first spurt of my cum coats her inner walls, I know there's no going back.

"No more running," I grunt, still coming.

Issy shudders beneath me, her tits heaving against my chest. "Yes, Daddy."

ISOBEL

I FALL ASLEEP TANGLED in Judah's arms. Unlike the first night we spent together, though, the panic never comes.

I feel relieved, scared, and worried, but also empowered. I made myself come, gave myself an earth-shattering orgasm on Judah's cock, and it was proof that everything I'd thought about myself was wrong. I'm not broken. I'm not frigid or unloveable. He's been trying to show me that since the day we met, and now I finally believe him.

At some point, when the first traces of early morning sunlight start to filter through the curtains, I stir at the feeling of his hard cock grinding against my ass. Neither of us says a word as Judah lifts my leg and guides himself into me in a single thrust that makes me cry out.

I'm swollen and tender from last night, but he goes slowly, two fingers circling my clit until I'm shaking and I finish with a cry. I'm still shaking from my release when Judah rolls us over, pinning me flat to the mattress as he pounds furiously into me, using my body for his pleasure, hissing out how good I feel, how tight, how he's going to fill me up.

"You want that, don't you, sweetheart?" he grits out in my ear, his whole body shaking with the effort not to fuck me too hard. "You want Daddy's cum deep in your tight little hole?"

His words send me over the edge for a second time, and he comes with me, his deep groans in my ear and the warmth of his release filling me.

We fall back asleep, but my alarm goes off not long after. I have to extract myself from a grumbling Judah's arms, murmuring that I'm going for a run and I'll see him later. I can't resist peaking over at him as I find my bikini and t-shirt, dressing quietly beside the bed. He looks so handsome like this, hair sticking up in every direction and lying sprawled beneath the tangled sheets. There are light scratches on his back from where my nails dug into him last night, and it's a very good thing all the family water activities have finally ended because those would be even harder to explain away than the bruises on my hips.

I'm falling for him, and it's like stepping out into the sun after years of staying in the shadows. Beautiful and exhilarating, but terrifying at the same time.

I'm still scared, however I've learned the hard way that running away isn't going to protect me from getting my heart broken. I spent all day yesterday helping arrange last-minute wedding details, stuffing gift bags, and listening to my mother's passive-aggressive criticism of everything from the appetizer trays to Reuben's shoes. Every word that came out of her mouth seemed to grate on me, and I felt sick with guilt over sneaking out on Judah.

Judah, who looks at me when I'm talking, who cares

about my opinion, and who makes me feel all the things I thought I couldn't.

Judah has gotten to know me better in five days than my mother has in twenty-three years.

Judah, whom I spent one day apart from and missed so much it hurt.

I have to force myself not to crawl back into bed with him, closing the door to his bungalow and hurrying down the walkway to my own. I'm tired and sore all over, and my thighs are sticky with Judah's cum, but I'm *so happy*. Or I am until I open my front door. I expect the room to be empty, but it isn't. My mother is seated in one of the plush white armchairs, watching me enter with an unreadable expression.

I close the door quietly behind me, mentally scrambling for any plausible explanation for me to be returning to my bungalow at seven in the morning wearing the same clothes as yesterday, looking like I spent the night being fucked into a mattress.

"You're up early," she observes coolly.

I clear my throat, looking anywhere but at her. I don't see why it matters to her if I'm sleeping with someone. She's never taken the slightest interest in my love life before this. She has no way of knowing it's Judah.

"I went for a walk."

Mom hums thoughtfully, leaning back in the chair and crossing her legs. "Don't lie to me, Isobel. You're dreadful at it. Tell me the truth. Now. Were you with someone?"

I don't really see a point in lying, so I nod. "Yes."

Her lips curl into a sneer. "Was it Judah Hale?"

My stomach drops as whatever grip I'd managed to keep on my anxiety is lost. How could she know? The panicked look must be as good as an admission to her

115

because Mom nods shortly, drumming her fingers on her knee. "I thought as much. You've been working very hard to make us look like horrible people with him, haven't you? He *attacked* your father last night because of whatever you've told him." She scoffs and gets to her feet, smoothing her linen dress. "You've had every opportunity in the world. We've given you every advantage in life, and still you resent us. Do you know why you aren't in the same position as your sister, Isobel? *Your feelings.*"

I don't reply. I can't, because my throat is tight and I can barely breathe. I don't want to hear this. Her cool indifference was one thing, but this...

Mom shakes her head, looking disgusted, as though she can hear everything I'm thinking and it's only proving her point. "Your inability to separate yourself from your emotions makes you *weak*, Isobel. Judah Hale is a powerful, well-respected man, and you reduce yourself to whispering lies in his ear and playing the damsel in distress to get his attention."

My eyes are burning, and my heart is broken, but I force myself to keep looking at her. She's throwing every horrible, hateful thing she can think of at me, and *it hurts*. It hurts so much, but with a dizzying burst of realization, I know she's *wrong*.

This woman is horrible, and she's wrong, and I'm so done giving her horrible, wrong words power over me. *Fuck. This.*

She's clearly about to keep going. Her eyes are narrowed and her thin lips are open, more hateful words poised on the tip of her tongue when I say, "Shut up."

Silence. Complete, ringing silence.

"What did you just say to me?" Mom asks after a long moment, her voice dangerously quiet.

I hold my head high and repeat, "I told you to *shut up*, Mom. I would rather be an emotional, anxious wreck every day of my life than be like you, and guess what else? I didn't have to tell Judah a *single thing* about you for him to see what kind of a person you are. He hates you because of *you*, not because of me."

Mom waits quietly until I'm done, staring at me with a soundless, cold fury burning behind her eyes. When I've finally fallen silent, my heart beating wildly, she walks slowly toward me. I see it coming, expect it, and still, I don't raise a hand to defend myself. A part of me wants it to happen.

My head turns with the force of her slap. As I straighten up, I touch my burning cheek in dazed disbelief. *She hit me.*

"Let me make myself very plain, Isobel Bradley," Mom says quietly, moving past me to the door. "If I get even an inkling that you're still seeing that man, or if you embarrass this family further in *any way*, you're on your own. No more support from your father or me, no more tuition money, no more apartment. Men like Judah get bored, and short-sighted little sluts who open their legs for them get thrown out like yesterday's trash."

I started running my sophomore year of college, right after having a very public panic attack in the middle of a final exam. My parents were furious, especially when the school psychologist *highly recommended* I take a semester off to focus on my mental health before returning. I was forced to return home, working at a local diner just to stay out of my parents' way, and I can't remember a time when I felt more broken. I started running to get out of the house, but it quickly became a way to work off frustration or stress.

I've never needed it more, though admittedly, crossing back over to Judah's bungalow and waking him up with my mouth around his cock was a good alternative. I need to think, though, and possibly ice my cheek because I'm pretty confident that if he saw me with a slap mark on my face, he would burn down the entire resort just to get at my mother.

Though she didn't go into details about what "attacking" Dad means, the fact that Mom deduced Judah and I are sleeping together from it leads me to believe that whatever he did was in my defense. The *only time* I've seen him angry has been at my parents for how they treat me.

He's been fighting for me since the first day we met.

I have to double over, gasping for air and clutching my burning thighs as I reach the end of the strip of beach I'm running on. Tears are blurring my vision, and for the first time in probably my whole life, they aren't from feeling bad things.

I'm in love with him.

He's the bossiest, most protective, sweetest man on the planet, and he wants *me*. I have no idea why or how I can possibly be good enough for him, but I can't keep those walls around my heart anymore. Not falling for Judah Hale is hard work, and I'm so damn tired.

I don't want to be a burden to him, though, and I don't want him to look at me as some kind of obligation. What will his friends and family think about a broke, homeless twenty-three-year-old crashing in his bed? That's what will happen if I don't fall in line with what my mom wants. God knows medical school is out now, which means all I'll have is a mostly finished bachelor's degree in a field I want nothing to do with and a few months of work experience as a waitress. The only thing in my life that I really love is volunteering at the daycare, but I don't have the necessary education to actually get a job there.

I'm so preoccupied and deep in thought that as I start running again, I almost miss the figure huddled on a lounge just under a towering palm tree. Movement catches my eye, though, and I turn, my heart dropping into the sand at the sight of Evie's tear-streaked face.

"Evie!" I gasp, hurrying over and dropping onto the lounge chair across from her. "What's wrong?"

She cries harder at my words, turning away so I can't see her. "I'm fine," she blubbers, shaking her head. "Really, Isobel. I'm just nervous about the wedding."

Normally, I would assume she doesn't want me around and keep running, but a voice in my head that sounds suspiciously like Judah keeps me glued to the spot. "Evie," I say cautiously, reaching out to squeeze her hand. "Is it Reuben? Are you guys alright?"

She lets out a watery laugh and finally turns to give me a pained smile. "Reuben is perfect. Really, Isobel, you don't have to stay. I've interrupted your run."

"I was getting tired anyway." I swing my legs up onto the lounge chair so we're reclining side by side. "I'll just sit with you if you want. It sucks to be alone when you're sad."

I'm trying to help, but apparently, I'm doing a terrible job because the moment the words have left my mouth, Evie bursts into tears all over again. "Stop being so nice to me." She gasps, shaking her head. "I don't deserve it."

I feel my mouth pop open and stare at her, at a complete loss to understand what's happening. "You're my sister. Of course, I'm going to be nice to you!"

Tears are streaming down her face, and she wipes them

away, her bottom lip trembling. "I don't deserve it, Isobel. I really, really don't."

I've never seen her look like this, and it's frankly alarming. "Just tell me what's going on. I'm sure we can fix whatever it is."

She looks over at me, her bottom lip trembling. "You're the best of us." She gives me a sad little smile. "Me, Mom, and Dad—we don't know how to stop. We have no idea how to connect. It took Reuben four years to convince me to go out with him because I was so focused on school. *Four years.* I'm so sorry you were stuck with us for your family."

My throat grows tight, and I look away, staring at the gently lapping ocean. "I think it's pretty clear who the weak link in the family is. I didn't... I didn't get into Weston. I found out the other day." It feels good to say it out loud. I haven't discussed it much, even with Judah, and telling Evie settles something inside me. *I'm not going to be a doctor.*

We sit together silently, staring out at the ocean for a long time. When Evie finally breaks the silence, her voice is full of shame. "I've been in therapy for about six months now. Reuben convinced me to go. It's been a lot. I've had to face a lot of stuff that I'd been pushing down for a long time. One of the big things is how shitty a sister I've been to you."

I curl my arms around my knees, keeping my eyes on the ocean. "Just because we aren't close doesn't mean you were shitty."

"I saw how Mom and Dad were treating you. I saw it, and I didn't do anything. You're my *little sister*, and I never protected you." Her voice breaks, and I finally find the courage to look at her, my eyes burning. Evie's eyes are on the waves, and she looks so tired and sad. "I did all these exercises with my therapist, thought of ways I could support you and show Mom and Dad I'm on your side. Then the minute we all get here, I become the same person I've always been. You're so much stronger than me." Her expression crumples. "I'm so sorry, Isobel."

I've wondered a lot about how Evie viewed me over the years, but it somehow never crossed my mind that she wanted to be my sister as badly as I wanted to be hers.

Wordlessly, I reach out to take her hand again. We sit that way for a long time. "I might not have been the best sister, either. Especially this week," I finally admit quietly, and Evie looks over at me with her lips pressed together to keep herself from smiling.

"Are you talking about Judah?"

I suck in a sharp breath, ripping my hand away from hers so I can grip the arm of the lounge chair and gape at her. "What?"

Evie laughs, wiping away the last of her tears. "You two aren't as subtle as you think you are. I wasn't sure, obviously, but there's a vibe."

"You're not pissed?"

"I hardly have the moral high ground, Isobel." She sighs heavily, shaking her head. "Besides, I get the appeal. From a purely aesthetic perspective."

I lean back in my chair, lost for words. Does *everyone* know? It's starting to feel like it. "I'm that obvious?"

"No." There's a smile in her voice. "You've been very stoic, but the way he looks at you is hard to miss. Reuben is pretty mortified, but he'll get over it. It's not just a hookup, right?"

"It's not just a hookup," I confirm, my whole heart full despite the awful confrontation with my mother. The further I ran, and the longer I sit here, the less her words hurt. I feel sorry for her because I don't think she's ever felt what I'm feeling right now or had someone look at her like Judah apparently looks at me.

In the space of a week, I've grown too big for her.

Evie nods slowly, her eyes on the horizon. "Do you want to be my maid of honor?"

I blink, positive I've misheard her. "What did you say?"

"Do you want to be my maid of honor?" she repeats, and she looks so vulnerable. "I understand if you don't want to or don't feel comfortable—"

"It's not that." I shake my head, still trying to process it. "I just didn't think you'd want me. What about your friends?"

Her hands twist together in her lap. "They're my bridesmaids. I wanted to ask you when we got here, but I've been so mixed up. I know I don't deserve a single thing from you, but—"

"I'd love to." My vision blurs with tears, and I wipe them away, smiling at my sister. "Though, I don't have a dress that matches the wedding colors."

Evie smiles sheepishly. "I have one for you. I thought, you know, just in case. You don't have to wear it if you don't want to. I swear I don't care."

My phone, which I strapped to my arm before leaving on my run, buzzes.

> Hot Guy from Airport Shuttle: Get your ass back here. I have a better workout for you.

I bite back a smile as I respond.

. . .

Isobel: Evie asked me to be her maid of honor! I'm going to help her get things ready for the rehearsal dinner.

Hot Guy from Airport Shuttle: That's amazing, Is. Have fun with your sister. Check in when you can?

Isobel: Maybe you should find me instead.

"What did you do to your cheek?"

I take my time putting my phone back in the carrier. I don't know how Evie, or Judah for that matter, would react if either knew what transpired between Mom and me, but the day before Evie and Reuben's wedding isn't the time to start an all-out family war. I need to navigate all this before getting anyone else involved.

"I think I slept on my hand," I finally tell Evie, though judging by her worried frown, she doesn't quite believe me.

FROM:	E.BRADLEY@COLUMBIAMED.COM
	C.HOLMESBRADLEY@NYCMED.COM, JBRADLEY@NYCMED.COM, R.HALE@COLUMBIAMED.COM, J.HALE@CDC.GOV, KENNEDY@LUCASREALTY.COM, NOLAN@LUCAS REALTY.COM, TOM@LUCASREALTY.COM, I.BRADLEY@UCHICAGO.EDU

SUBJECT: DAY 6: ITINERARY OVERVIEW

The rehearsal dinner is tonight. Info is on your invitations. I'm done with these, I'm sure you're all capable of figuring out the rest of this on your own.

E

thirteen

JUDAH

I HAD no idea how many people Evie and Reuben invited to this wedding until I started spotting second cousins I haven't seen since high school next to the pool. Then I see my Great-Uncle Otis complaining loudly to the reception desk about how someone left towels folded on his bed—when he called weeks ago to inform them he would be bringing his own.

Apparently, not many people could resist a tropical vacation, though I highly doubt Reuben warned Caroline or Evie that most of mine and Kennedy's families have never left Kentucky before and aren't exactly going to mesh well with the buttoned-up Bradley contingent.

I run into so many distant relatives who pull me into conversations that even though I leave a full hour before the official start of the rehearsal dinner, I arrive in the resort's luxury dining room only fifteen minutes early. I narrowly avoid running headlong into a harassed-looking Reuben as I walk inside. He still isn't dressed, and his hair is sticking up like he's been running his hand through it. "Run. Save yourself," he mutters darkly, edging around me and glancing back to where Kennedy, Caroline, Evie, and Isobel are organizing favor bags in stilted silence.

"What's going on?"

Reuben grimaces. "Well if I had to guess, I'd say it has something to do with you choking John in the middle of the resort lounge because he insulted your girlfriend. Though, to be fair, the resort also fucked up a bunch of details for the reception tomorrow, so that didn't exactly raise spirits. They haven't said a word to each other in over an hour. It's been a nightmare. I'm just now running back to change."

To illustrate the point, Caroline crisply asks Evie to pass the tissue paper even though it's right in front of Isobel.

Christ.

I wince. The cat is well and truly out of the bag, and I have no one to blame but myself. I don't regret it, but I hate that I put Issy in that situation and disregarded Reuben's request to keep the wedding drama-free. "I'm sorry it went down the way it did. It wasn't my intention to cause problems."

"It's not your fault." Reuben sighs wearily, craning his neck around me to check on Evie. "Well, it's mostly not your fault. This certainly didn't help matters, but god knows this started a long time before you or I came along. On the bright side, I think Evie got to talk to Isobel because she finally asked her to be our maid of honor."

My chest fills with emotion, knowing how much that undoubtedly meant to Issy. "I heard."

Reuben is watching me, frowning. "I won't ask if this is just a fling or whatever because I know you wouldn't do that. Be careful, though, Dad. She's a lot younger than you. I don't want to see you get hurt. She might just be having fun—"

"She isn't," I cut him off firmly. I appreciate the sentiment, and I'm proud as hell of the kind of man he's grown to be, but I know what I'm doing. This might be uncharted territory for me, but I know I won't be letting that woman go. Like she can feel me looking at her, Issy looks up, her eyes widening when she sees me standing across the room in my tux. Fuck, if that isn't good for my ego.

I need to get her alone, though. I put her in a shitty position with her parents, and her naked appearance in my shower last night drove every other thought from my head. She's anxious now, I can tell, and I hate that I had any part in making her feel that way.

Reuben, oblivious to the look exchanged between Issy and me, still looks mortified even to be having this discussion. "I honestly can't believe it. You're normally the sensible one in the family."

Ha. I am. Though, my recent lack of sense isn't my biggest problem right now. I just want to get Issy alone and find out what's happened.

"I'll take over," I offer, gripping his shoulder bracingly. "Go get dressed."

Reuben eyes me skeptically. "You want to sit in a room and play mediator between your daughter-in-law, the college student you're apparently seeing, and their mother? Oh, and also your ex-wife."

As he speaks, Evie says something under her breath to Issy before the two head in our direction, Caroline watching them go with narrowed eyes and pinched lips.

I ignore her, too preoccupied with staring at how the hem of Issy's strappy black cocktail dress flutters danger-ously close to the bottom of her sweet little ass. It would be too fucking easy to bend her over, tug her panties to the side and fuck my cum into her for the second time today. I feel a flash of regret for not examining her pussy after what we did. Some primal, possessive part of me wants to know what she looks like, her little hole swollen and red from taking my too big cock, my cum dripping down her thighs.

Just thinking about it makes heat bloom deep inside me, and Issy's steps falter as they approach, no doubt seeing the hungry look on my face.

"Reuben!" Evie admonishes when they get close, gesturing to his shorts and t-shirt with wide, disbelieving eyes. "What are you doing? You need to be dressed!"

He holds up his hands and backs away toward the door. "I'm going!"

Evie looks beautiful, her dark hair arranged in loose curls around her shoulders and dressed in a peach-colored gown. I should probably be complimenting the bride, but I can't stop looking at the little tease beside her. I've never seen Issy wear anything more formal than a sundress. She takes my breath away on an hourly basis just by existing. How the fuck am I supposed to get through this dinner without putting my hands on her when she's wearing black satin and stilettos so high they make her legs look endless?

She isn't looking at me, though, and I feel a flash of fear that I might have gone too far last night. Her parents might be assholes, but they're her *parents*, and I've complicated an already tangled situation. I open my mouth to ask her to talk to me alone, but Caroline calls out behind us before I can.

"Isobel! You should be leaving to walk your grand-mother over here!"

Issy hurries off without a word, and I have to grit my teeth to keep myself from snapping at Caroline. It won't help, and I need to find out what's going on in her head before making any big moves. I'd thought everything was fine, but now... I move to follow her, but Evie catches my elbow, and I look around at her.

"Don't," she warns me under her breath, darting her eyes toward Caroline. "You'll make it worse."

"What's going on?"

Evie shakes her head, lips pinched in worry. "I'm really not sure. I think she and Mom had some kind of fight this morning, probably about you. Neither of them are talking though, and—"

"Oh, Donald, look how grown she is. Little Evie, a bride!" I step out of the way as an old woman barrels past me in a cloud of perfume, engulfing Evie in a hug I can smell from here.

"Aunt Janice." Evie's smile looks painful. "Thank you so much for coming. Reuben just had to run back to his bungalow, but this is his father, Judah."

I help Evie greet the first wave of guests before Reuben reappears to take over. I'm trying to decide whether I should leave in search of Issy or wait for her to come to me when she enters the room beside a sour-faced old woman who must be her grandmother.

"Much too short. I don't know why women feel the need to show so much skin," the woman grumbles disapprovingly, shaking her head as they approach Evie and Reuben. "Evelyn, my goodness. Your mother let you keep your hair that long for the wedding?"

Issy makes her escape, meeting my eyes as she strides across the slowly filling room, slipping outside onto the empty patio. I take the hint, following her after a quick look confirming that Caroline is occupied with her newly arrived mother and John is nowhere in sight.

I find her waiting in a shadowy corner, her expression unreadable.

"Hey," I say cautiously as I approach, but she doesn't let me worry for long. My chest relaxes when she moves forward, wrapping her arms around my middle tightly and burying her face in my chest.

We're okay.

"What's going on?" I ask, kissing her hair. It feels so good to hold her like this and know she's looking to me for comfort. "Reuben said things have been tense."

"It's a long story." She snuggles closer, relaxing slightly as I run my hand back and forth over her back. "You look really good in a tux, by the way."

I chuckle. "If you're a good girl, I'll let you take it off later. Dinner isn't going to start for a few minutes. We have time. Tell me now."

Issy pulls away with a sigh. While she doesn't look angry, I can feel anxiety and tension radiating off her as she begins to speak. "My mom was waiting for me when I got back to my bungalow this morning. I guess she put the pieces together after you *attacked* my father? Why did you do that?"

My stomach drops. "I'm so sorry, Issy. I never meant to put you in that position. I should have told you what happened last night, but..." I trail off, trying to find a way to say I was distracted by her pussy without sounding like a hormonal teenager.

"It's okay. I'm sure he was being a dick." She shrugs helplessly, looking away toward the ocean. "Mom was mad. She said a lot of stuff, and I guess I'm just processing. I'll figure it out."

"*We* will," I correct.

She heaves a sigh, looking back at me wearily. "Listen, I think we need to take a step back. *For now*. Things are tense, and I need to play by Mom's rules until I finish college."

I stare at her, my whole body suddenly numb. "What did she say to you?"

"It doesn't matter."

"Yes. It does." I step forward, crowding her into the railing, and hear her breath catch. "Because you don't want to take steps back, do you?"

Issy blinks up at me, clearly trying to keep a grasp on whatever resolution she came to in the hours we've been apart. "I—*Yes*. I do."

"Haven't you figured out by now that I know when you're lying, Isobel Bradley?" I drop my head forward, kissing her fluttering pulse point. "Things like this, *like us*, don't happen every day. You gave yourself to me last night, and you can't take it back now."

My hand dips beneath the short hem of her dress, gripping her whole pussy through the damp panties she's wearing. Issy whimpers, her eyes going wide. "Judah, I'm just saying we should be logical with the wedding—"

"Fuck logical." I hook her panties to the side and push two fingers inside her. She's still swollen from the last few days. I've been rough on her, but the soft, needy whine she makes when I add a third finger is proof she needs it like that. I'm going to have my hands full, keeping her needy cunt satisfied. "We agreed, Issy. No more running. What the hell are you doing?" I fuck her slowly with measured strokes of my fingers, my thumb gently circling her stiff little nub as wetness coats my hand.

It's intoxicating how quickly her body always responds to me.

"*Daddy*." Her hands tighten on my tux, grinding her pussy to get more from me.

"The wedding will be over by this time tomorrow." I hook my fingers into her G-spot, swallowing her cry with a searing kiss. "Evie and Reuben know, and they don't give a shit. This is about your asshole parents."

She's close. Her inner walls are fluttering around my fingers, and her breath is coming in feverish pants. I stop, pulling my fingers from beneath her dress and sucking her sweet cream away while she watches, outraged.

"Judah!"

"*Issy.*" I chuckle, reaching back between her legs to pull her panties back into place and give her cloth-covered cunt a sharp little spank. "I left my bungalow unlocked. I want you waiting for me when I get back tonight, on all fours, naked at the edge of the bed. I'm going to fill that little pussy with my cum, and then you're going to talk to me."

ISOBEL

I COULD GO BACK to my own bungalow. I know that. Giving myself some space would be good, allow me to get my thoughts in order after yet another day of ups and downs. Yet as the rehearsal dinner begins to wind down at the end of the night, I still find myself turning off the dock to Judah's.

He was still standing with a group of my father's cousins when I left the resort's restaurant. I felt his eyes follow me to the door, though, and have no doubt he won't be far behind. I've been tense and on edge all day, avoiding my parents like the plague but somehow ending up near them again and again. They still don't know I didn't get into Weston, and I have no doubt shit will well and truly hit the fan when it inevitably comes out.

I'm not afraid of them cutting me off financially or never speaking to me again. Both sound like a relief at this point, but I can't dismiss the fear that this will all be too much for Judah. We haven't talked about the future, not really, and while the connection between us is undeniable, does he know what he's getting himself into?

We're in paradise right now. Will he still want me in the real world?

I don't bother turning on the lights when I close the door behind me, walking straight through to the dark bedroom and stripping naked, just like he asked. It's a relief to focus on something other than my own fear and worry, to take my mind out of the equation and surrender control to Judah. By the time I've crawled onto the bed, waiting on my hands and knees with my legs spread for him, I can barely remember why I was so upset to begin with.

The longer I wait, the more worked up I get. When the front door finally closes quietly a few minutes later, my wetness is beginning to drip down my thighs.

"Good girl." I tremble, fighting the urge to peek over my shoulder as Judah's footsteps move slowly into the room, stopping just behind me. His hands reach out to touch my hips, steadying me. "You needed this, didn't you? Needed Daddy to take control?"

I nod, my ears ringing as his big hands slide back to my ass, spreading me open so he can see everything.

"I'm going to fuck your ass one day." He runs one finger teasingly over my puckered back entrance, and I whimper, squeezing my eyes shut. "I popped your cherry with my fingers two days ago. Now look at you, waiting in the dark, desperate for your old man to fuck you."

I can barely breathe as his hands fall away, and I hear the soft clink of a belt being undone. *Yes, yes, yes—*

"Tell me why you're feeling so anxious." One of his hands finds my hips, holding me steady as his stiff length presses against my entrance.

My eyelids flutter, and it's a struggle to concentrate on the feelings and worries that had seemed too real to me only a few minutes ago. "I-I'm worried you won't want me after we leave here. My mother, she—*oh god.*"

He's guiding the head of his cock over my oversensitive clit in firm circles. I moan loudly, trying to come back for more, but the hand on my hip keeps me from thrusting against him. It's torture. "Keep going."

"She said that she and Dad wouldn't pay for my college or apartment or anything if I kept seeing you. She said a lot of other things, awful things, but I don't care anymore. I just, I worried—"

Judah's hand tightens reflexively on my hip, and his voice is low and full of warning when he answers after a long pause. "What the fuck does that have to do with me wanting you?"

I stare down at my hands clutching the rumpled white sheets, tears swimming in my eyes. "I don't have a job or money. I won't be able to finish my degree. I don't know what I'm going to do if I don't go to medical school. And all that is *on top* of the issues with my family and me being half your age and an anxious basket case. Why would you want to be with someone like that?" A tear hits the sheets below me. "I'm not good enough for you."

In a week full of vulnerable, tough moments, this one is by far the hardest. If he realizes I'm right and he walks away now...

Without warning, Judah thrusts forward, burying himself inside me with a harsh grunt. I cry out, my already sore muscles protesting the sudden intrusion, but he doesn't give me time to adjust. I'm completely open to him like this, and I feel him hit the deepest part of me over and over again, unrelenting and brutal. He's punishing me with his cock.

"Do you want to know what I see when I look at you?" A

big hand closes around my throat, pressing hard enough for my breath to come in shallow pants and stars to burst in front of my eyes. Judah growls, hunched forward over me, and I realize he's still wearing his tux. "I see a fucking miracle, Isobel Bradley. You're kind and good and loyal. Those people—they don't see you, love. It's bullshit, and I'd give anything to spare you that pain, but neither of us can change what's broken in them."

Tears are flowing steadily down my cheeks now, and I let out a noise somewhere between a laugh and a sob when the angle of Judah's thrusts changes so his cock is rubbing right against my G-spot. My orgasm comes out of nowhere, powerful enough that my arms grow weak, and only Judah's hand on my throat keeps me from falling face-first into the mattress. He's everywhere; there's not a single piece of me I can hide from this man, and I don't want to.

"Oh god," I cry, the aftershocks of my orgasm still surging through my body as he pulls out and flips me over, reentering me with a low groan of pleasure. He's so handsome that just looking at him steals my breath all over again, and I reach up to grab his tux, dragging him down to kiss me greedily.

Three days ago, I'd never had an orgasm, and now I'm naked beneath a fully dressed, much older man, my pussy stretched around his thick cock.

"You like it when Daddy takes you rough, don't you, sweetheart? Like feeling me use your little hole?" Judah growls in my ear, his pace faltering slightly when I clench the muscles of my sex to make myself tighter for him. "*Tell me.*"

I feel more wetness flooding over his cock. "Yes, Daddy!"

"*Fuck*, Is." He ducks his head, kissing and biting my

neck and breasts as his thrusts become shallow and frantic. He's close. "You're mine now. Do you hear me, sweetheart? *Mine.* I'll want you until they put me in the ground. Do you believe me?"

I nod, clinging to him as fresh tears pour down the sides of my face, and Judah stills above me, his cock shoved deep inside me, spilling.

"I'm going to get you pregnant," he whispers, voice rough with emotion. "Going to give you a family, Issy. A *real* family. I've always wanted that, and I think you have too. So, we're going to make one together."

He's right.

He's still inside me, softening, and our heartbeats are just starting to slow when I begin to laugh. It's a hysterical, joyful sound that I'm absolutely positive I've never made before. Like all these things I'm feeling are so big they can't be contained inside me anymore. "I'm in love with you. Like, *really* in love with you." I laugh some more, staring up into Judah's face. He looks like I'm feeling: *awed.*

One hand cradles my jaw as he leans forward to kiss me, silencing my laughs. I'll never get used to how good it feels to touch him like this or feel connected to another person. "I'm in love with you too, Issy," Judah murmurs when we finally break apart, pressing his forehead to mine. "All that shit? School and work and your family? We will figure it out. I want you as is."

He's right. Who we are and the things we want, those are the most important. Everything else is just details.

fifteen

JUDAH

REUBEN AND EVIE'S wedding day begins with the news that John and Caroline left late last night.

The official reason that's been circulated throughout the extended family is that the wife of a dear friend needed surgery, and John happens to be an expert in the procedure. Apparently, Evie gave her wholehearted support and begged her parents to leave early. The less official reason, known only to the bride, groom, maid of honor, and myself, is that Evie asked them to leave.

"Evie and Caroline had it out about Isobel last night after the dinner," Reuben informs me under his breath as we stand off to the side, watching guests begin to take their seats on the beach for the ceremony. "Caroline wouldn't take accountability for anything and John tried to jump in to defend her, but Evie shut it down. She accused Caroline of slapping Isobel when she found out about the two of you. When Caroline confirmed it, she told them she didn't want them here." There's unmistakable pride in his voice, but just the thought sends a sharp stab of regret through me.

Issy told me about the confrontation with her mother late last night, with the agreement that I wouldn't do or say anything about it to her parents until the wedding was over for Evie's and Reuben's sakes. I've felt so fucking guilty that my actions caused that, but my daughter-in-law ensured some good came out of it. John and Caroline didn't deserve to be here for either of their daughters, and I'm ridiculously proud of them.

"You couldn't have done better. That's one hell of a wife you've found," I tell Reuben, looking back toward where the last guests seem to be taking their seats. I didn't think today would make me feel like this, but I've been a sappy mess since I woke up. My son is getting married today. When I got that invitation months ago, it felt like the end of something, like my window for happiness had closed and it was all downhill from here.

I was so wrong it's almost comical. This isn't the end at all, it's a new beginning, and I'm so full of joy and hope I physically can't wipe the smile off my face.

The officiant nods to Reuben, who gives me one last tight hug before going to stand beneath the chuppah, his groomsmen following. I sit beside Kennedy and Tom in the front row just as quiet classical music begins to play, and all the guests' hushed voices fall away. They couldn't have timed the ceremony better. The sun is just starting to set, and the sky is painted pink and orange.

Evie's bridesmaids come first, dressed in gold and holding bouquets of white orchids.

I don't realize I'm holding my breath until Issy appears at the end of the aisle, and all the air rushes out of me. Her hair is braided loosely over one shoulder, and she's wearing a longer version of the satin dress all the bridesmaids wear.

She's beaming and so fucking beautiful I have to remind myself to blink. I keep thinking about what she told me last night about her worries that she isn't good enough for me or that I'll regret her.

Isobel Bradley has given me everything—her love, her trust, her future, and it's *me* who shouldn't feel worthy.

As she passes me and takes her place beside the chuppah, she grins over her shoulder before winking right at me, and I feel Kennedy stiffen.

"I thought it was my imagination." She huffs under her breath as the music changes, and we get to our feet. "*Really*, Judah? I liked her for Nolan."

I bite back a laugh, glancing at her youngest son, who stands beside Reuben as best man. Even now, he keeps glancing hopefully over at Issy, obviously wondering if any of the best man–maid of honor stereotypes will hold true. I can't say I blame him; she's the most radiant woman I've ever seen, but unfortunately for Nolan, she's looking right at me.

The crowd murmurs when Evie appears at the end of the aisle, practically glowing in her simple white gown. Since John left last night, she's alone, but not for long. Reuben reaches her before she's made it even a quarter of the way up the aisle and kisses her deeply right there. Some people laugh, but mostly I see shining eyes and watery smiles as the bride and groom make their way back up the aisle together.

* * *

Somewhere between the ceremony and the reception, I lose track of Issy.

Reuben and Evie are swarmed by well-wishers when they enter the room, and I barely had a chance to congratulate them before being bumped out of the way by heavily perfumed Aunt Janice. I'm about to head to the bar when I catch sight of a single figure in the distance, lingering on the beach behind where the ceremony was held with her feet in the water.

"So, when does your flight leave?" I call as I approach. Issy turns around, smiling at me.

"If my mother hasn't canceled it?" she scoffs, shaking her head. "Tomorrow afternoon. Yours?"

"The same, actually." We haven't discussed what comes next, but these particular *details* suddenly feel very important to work out. I reach her, and the tension leaves my shoulders as she twines her arms around my neck, pulling me down for a kiss. "I've been thinking you should change your travel arrangements."

Her eyebrows lift in mock surprise. "Oh? What did you have in mind?"

"Your spring semester doesn't start for a few weeks, right?" It's not really a question. I looked up her university's schedule last night after she fell asleep, a hot ball of dread settling in my stomach at the thought of doing the long-distance thing for months.

Issy's lips press together to stop herself from smiling. "I think I'm going to take some time off. Finishing a pre-med degree doesn't seem like a great use of my time, considering I hate the idea of going into medicine. No offense, Doc."

"None taken." I laugh, slapping her ass playfully and dragging her closer. "So, *hypothetically speaking*, what do you think about coming to D.C. instead?"

"Hypothetically?" She hums, sliding her hands down to straighten my shirt collar. "That sounds amazing."

142

I arch my eyebrows, surprised. "No arguments?"

"Nope." She smiles, and I weave our fingers together and kiss the back of her hand. My heart is so fucking full it hurts. "I'll have to go back to Chicago to clear out my apartment. I should probably get a storage unit or something."

"I have space." The thought of all her stuff mixed with mine satisfies some primal, possessive part of me. There are zero areas of my life where I don't want her. Issy doesn't argue, and wordlessly she tugs me back toward the wedding reception.

If anyone has an opinion or disapproves of the groom's father holding hands with the bride's sister, I don't notice. Someone—probably Evie—changed the place settings so we're seated together, and when a few of my cousins come over to say hello, I introduce them to my girlfriend. The moment they leave, though, I frown at her.

Issy, who's just finished stealing a slice of cucumber off my plate and popping it into her mouth, stares back at me questioningly. "What's wrong?"

"I don't like it," I admit, looking off to where Reuben is proudly introducing his new wife to a childhood friend.

The word *girlfriend* seems insufficient to describe how much I love this woman or the level of devotion I feel for her. *Girlfriend* feels temporary, but Issy is forever.

She leans her head on my shoulder and helps herself to another piece of cucumber. "We're moving in together after a week, Judah. I think that suggests things are pretty serious."

It does, but I'm still not satisfied. "I don't suppose you'd marry me before we leave? Wife sounds pretty good."

She laughs, shaking her head against me. "You suppose correctly, Doctor Hale. Let Evie and Reuben have their big day. Besides, did it ever occur to you that maybe I want to wear a big white dress and boss everyone around"

It didn't. "You want a big wedding?"

"Maybe." I kiss her head, and she sighs happily. Across the room, the band has called everyone's attention to Reuben and Evie's first dance. "I'd like to know the groom's middle name before making any big decisions on the guest list."

"It's Charles." I snort, pulling her closer. We watch in silence for a while as the newlyweds dance, wrapped up in each other and so clearly in love. "Did you talk to Evie about what happened with your parents?"

"A little," she admits. "There was some crying earlier this morning, but I think she feels good about standing up to them. I never really thought about how hard it must have been for her to try and be perfect all the time. We agreed that we need to start over and figure out who we are without our parents' filters, if that makes any sense."

Fuck, just when I thought I couldn't fall any harder for this woman.

"It does." The song has ended, and people are flooding onto the dimly lit dance floor. I stand and offer Issy my hand, tugging her gently back to her feet and through the other couples until we find a space. It feels so good to hold her like this, in the middle of a wedding packed with our relatives, without the slightest hint of fear or worry. Some people might judge us, but there's no opinion in the world that I care about more than my girl's happiness.

"I hope we come back here someday." Issy sighs, looking outside to where the dark ocean is just barely visible. "I'll miss it."

I love the idea of spending time here with just her. No family, no struggling with our feelings, just time to enjoy each other. "We'll come back for our honeymoon," I promise.

Issy looks up at me, and she looks so carefree and beautiful that it takes my breath away. "Don't you think you should learn my middle name before signing up for that kind of commitment?"

"No." I laugh. "Tell me anyway. It might be useful."

epilogue

ONE YEAR **Later**

When we reach the airport shuttle, the very same driver who once hit on my now-wife is waiting to take us to the resort.

If he recognizes us, he doesn't give any indication of it. I have to bite back a smile, tucking Issy closer against my side when we settle into the thankfully air-conditioned back seat. So much has changed in the past year, but how I feel when I touch her isn't one of them. She still takes my breath away daily and, while I keep expecting the honeymoon phase to fade away or to start taking the little things for granted, it hasn't happened yet.

"We'll lay down when we get there," I promise, kissing the crown of her hair as she nestles closer. I called the resort twice to confirm we'd be staying in the same bungalow I did last year. I have big plans to fuck her ass for the first time in the place where I once took her virginity and enjoy all the benefits of being in such a beautiful place with the woman I love *without* our families.

Our last time here, things were so complicated and

intense. This trip, my only plans are to spoil the hell out of my wife and fuck her senseless. God knows we won't be making it back anytime soon.

At the thought, I reach over and press my hand over the swell of her belly. This trip was originally supposed to be nearly three months ago, right after our wedding, but I was firmly against international air travel while Issy was in her first trimester.

The pregnancy wasn't planned. Granted, our birth control methods have always been questionable at best. Considering my profession, I really shouldn't have been surprised, but I was.

One ordinary Tuesday morning, I opened an exam room door, expecting to let a new patient know that her blood work had come back to confirm a first-trimester pregnancy. Instead, I found my fiancée sitting on the table wearing the world's biggest smile, her eyes shining with tears.

My entire staff was in on it and were waiting outside the room for us to emerge, ecstatic and holding a grainy ultrasound showing *two* tiny heartbeats.

The constant paranoia is another unexpected byproduct of being a soon-to-be new father—for the first time in almost thirty years—and a physician. I know all too well the horrible things that could go wrong, endangering my wife's and our babies' lives. I'm being overprotective and overbearing, and while I've certainly gotten some well-deserved eye rolls, Issy seems to be taking it all in stride.

Normally, she's the tense one, but this pregnancy seems to have brought on a role reversal between us. With every passing week, Issy gets happier and more content while I keep waking up in the middle of the night to research completely ordinary pregnancy symptoms. I'm determined to enjoy this trip, though.

"You're on vacation Doctor Hale." Issy pokes my side. "Put the frown away."

I am frowning, aren't I?

"I'm sorry." I reach into the carry-on bag at my feet and pull out a water bottle, handing it to her. "Drink something. You slept for most of the last flight."

She rolls her eyes but does as I ask just as the shuttle slows, pulling up outside the resort's lobby. "Do you think I should check in with Judy?" she asks as I get up and help her down onto the sidewalk, unable to stop myself from running my eyes over her beautiful curves.

Between preparing for the trip, a last-minute visit to Evie and Reuben, and a hectic work schedule for both of us, we haven't had sex in over a week. It's unprecedented. I don't remember the last time we went longer than a few days at most. Unfortunately, this little dry spell has over-lapped with her belly becoming suddenly much more noticeable.

I'm always wildly attracted to my wife, but seeing her body grow with my babies is the sexiest thing I've ever seen. I want her constantly, and while I know I should let her sleep when we get to the bungalow, all I can think about is how she'd look spread out on that big white bed, begging Daddy to eat her sweet pussy.

"Judah?"

I snap out of the fantasy, blinking at Issy, who looks like she's trying not to laugh. "I'm sorry, what?"

She giggles and weaves her fingers through mine, tugging me toward the lobby. "I asked if you thought I should check in with Judy."

"She's got it. You're on vacation too, Mrs. Hale."

A few months after moving in together, I mentioned that a lot of my patients have to bring their young children in for their appointments because they don't have childcare and how distracting or stressful it can be.

My wife, the incredible creature she is, showed up at the office the next day with a box of toys, coloring books, and crayons for our receptionist to give to all the mothers who come through with their kids. A few weeks later, she tentatively asked if she could volunteer at my clinic, offering free childcare for my patients at their appointments.

Now, nearly a year in, the practice just hired our first full-time childcare employee, and what was once a storage room has been converted into a playroom. The results have been incredible: relaxed patients, fewer cancellations, and we can fit more appointments since the schedule is running faster. It's worked so well that a few of my colleagues have hired her to consult on adding the service at their practices.

My wife is brilliant, compassionate, and kind.

As we walk into the lobby, my heart swells with nostalgia. Our lives have changed so much since we were last here, and it's almost bizarre to come back and find everything the same as it was a year ago. Not all the memories are good. Caroline and John are, and likely always will be, a very raw wound for Issy.

In the days and weeks after the wedding, rumors started coming out.

The Bradleys are well known throughout the medical community. I'd prepared myself for a certain degree of blowback for leaving D.C. a single man and returning with a twenty-three-year-old live-in girlfriend who happens to be my son's sister-in-law.

It says a lot that the most interesting gossip to come out of the weekend wasn't about me and Issy at all.

Apparently, the big fight Evie had with them the night of the rehearsal dinner was in the restaurant after the end of the party. Unfortunately for Caroline and John, Dr. Franklin, a colleague of theirs, had returned to get her forgotten phone and overheard the entire thing. The highlights spread like wildfire, which led to a whole group of former residents filing a formal complaint against both of them for hostile and abusive work environments.

I can only assume lawsuits were threatened because, by some miracle, neither lost their jobs. The damage was done, though. Their reputations, the most important thing in the world to Caroline and John, are ruined.

I know Evie has sporadic contact with them, but Issy hasn't spoken to either since the wedding. I'm not sure they even know she's pregnant. Standing in this room, it's impossible not to remember how broken Issy was when we met and to feel that anger toward them all over again.

Most days, when we're curled in bed, it's easy to forget that it wasn't always like this. Our new normal is me making her laugh, or her teasing me about how much creamer I put in my coffee, or bickering over where to go for dinner.

I won't be the one to remind her, though. Not now. She's glowing with happiness, and despite sitting on a plane for the better part of twenty-four hours and two small humans making her crave weird food and throw up whenever she smells eggs, she's still the most beautiful woman I've ever seen.

Thankfully, check-in doesn't take long, and we follow the porter through the resort to our bungalow.

"It hasn't changed," Issy declares happily, beaming at me over her shoulder once we're finally inside.

Determined to shake off my suddenly dark mood, I tug her back into my arms, kissing her reverently. Just her lips on mine is enough to send heat rushing to my cock all over again, and I gather her closer, pressing my erection into her stomach to show her what she does to me.

I draw back, smirking. "Take your clothes off."

Issy bites her lip. "I'm pretty tired. Can we take a nap first?"

I back off, immediately ashamed of myself. My pregnant wife has just traveled around the world. She needs rest, not me grinding my dick all over her. "Of course. I'm sorry, sweetheart."

"Don't be sorry." She kisses me once more, briefly, before heading off to the bathroom to clean up, and I wander into the bedroom to flop down on the bed. I'm too keyed up from traveling to sleep now, but I'll happily hold her while she does.

Taking the opportunity to touch base with Reuben, I pull out my phone and send him a quick text.

> Judah: Hey! Just letting you know we arrived safely.

> Reuben: Good to hear! Evie is jealous. Make sure you tell my stepmother to send her some pics.

I snort. If the worst grief my son gives me for marrying a woman younger than him is some lighthearted stepmother jokes, I won't complain.

I'm about to ask if they have any souvenir requests when the bathroom door slides smoothly open, and I have what can only be described as a small stroke. That's the only explanation for why my mouth is hanging open, unable to form words, and all conscious thoughts have been completely wiped from my mind.

Issy is standing in the doorway, her lips curled into a dangerous little smile. She's dressed in a white lace corset that covers her rib cage, stopping just above her swollen belly, and a pair of matching panties that are molded over her perfect cunt. The material is dotted with tiny flowers, and she somehow manages to look sexy and innocent at the same time.

Holy fuck.

"I'm not actually that tired." Issy giggles, moving further into the room and crawling onto the end of the bed. The last time I saw her naked, a few days ago, she had a cute little strip of hair over her mound. That's gone now, and I can see every inch of her beautiful skin through the flimsy material.

I exhale heavily, my cock already painfully hard. Palming it through my shorts, I watch her move forward, straddling my calf. "Not tired, huh?" I finally manage to ask, my voice strained. "Are you horny, sweetheart?"

Issy nods, biting her lip to keep from smiling. She lowers her hips, grinding her pussy over my leg as she squeezes her own breasts. She is every filthy, depraved fantasy I've ever had.

"Come here." I crook my finger at her, and she crawls

forward immediately, settling her hot slit over my erection. There are two layers of clothing between us, but I can still feel how wet she is. My little wife loves teasing me. "Did you wear this to get Daddy's attention?" I pluck at the little bow resting just over her mound.

In response, my greedy girl starts to roll her hips, eyelashes fluttering. I let her have her fun for a moment, but then a sharp spank to her bare ass makes her gasp, hips faltering.

"I asked you a question."

She nods immediately. "Yes, Daddy."

I hum approvingly, running my hands over her firm belly to replace her touch with my own, pinching her nipples roughly. I'm so goddamn hard that if she doesn't stop grinding on me like that, I'm going to spill in my fucking pants.

Careful of her belly, I roll us over so she's sprawled beneath me. Her panties are soaked and sticking to her cunt. "Christ, this is so hot." I hook her panties out of the way and trace my fingers over the soft, bare skin I uncover, making her squirm and whimper.

"*Daddy*—"

"Shhh," I hush, ripping my t-shirt over my head in one fluid movement. "I'll give you what you need, sweetheart." I love to tease her, fucking adore making her beg and whine for me to fill her up, but not today.

My hands move to the button on my shorts, and a few seconds later, my cock is free, the head finding her entrance like a damn magnet. Even after a year, it still takes some work for me to get inside her tightness. Usually, I try to ease her into it. Right now, though, she has me too fucking worked up to stop and finger her.

A scream tears from her lips as I punch forward, burying myself balls deep in her wet heat.

"This is what you get for teasing," I growl, turned on by how her eyes widen as I begin to fuck her, slow and deep. It's intoxicating, the feeling of her body gripping mine and how gloriously wet she always gets for me. Every fucking time. "Do you need more?"

She nods immediately, her legs tightening around my back, trying to pull me deeper. "It feels so good. *Oh, god.* Judah!"

My name on her lips makes me groan. I fuck her harder, making her tits bounce and her hands clutch my shoulders, holding on for dear life. My balls are already tightening, threatening to spill, but she's going to come first.

"Touch your clit," I grit out, my thighs burning from the workout they're getting. There are still some days when we stay in bed for hours, teasing and exploring, making each other come over and over again. More often than not, though, we're so desperate that there's no holding back.

Like now.

Issy's hand moves between us just as I change the angle of my thrusts, hitting the spot I know will make her come hard and fast. Sure enough, her throaty cry comes only a few seconds later, and the feeling of her inner walls clamping down on my shaft sends me over the edge too. The pleasure is so intense that it's all I can do not to collapse on top of her, my cock still twitching inside her, filling her.

Fuck, I needed that.

"Christ, you're so sexy." I groan as I pull out, falling to the mattress beside her. "Was I too rough?"

Issy shakes her head, rolling onto her side so she's

facing me, that beautiful little bump between us. "No, that was perfect. I needed it too. Thank you, baby."

I chuckle, plucking at the sheer material she's wearing. "I should be thanking you. When did you get this?"

"Before the wedding," she admits with a little giggle. "I didn't know it would take so long for me to wear it, though, or that your twins would ruin the innocent bridal effect I was going for. Look." She rolls slightly, and I can see she had to cut a slit in the back of the corset to accommodate her growing belly. "Does it look ridiculous?"

"No," I reply instantly, giving her a sharp little spank for suggesting it. "I'm going to request you wear it later too."

She rolls her eyes, but she's glowing with such obvious happiness that it fills me up too. "Don't worry, there's *lots* more where this came from. But we flew around the world to come here, husband. Don't you want to experience more than this bedroom?"

"I have my gorgeous, pregnant wife alone for ten whole days. Do you think I care where we are? I'd fuck you on the moon and be just as happy."

Issy's body shakes with laughter. "Come on, you loved that seafood place."

I sit back on my heels and spread her legs wide, grinning wickedly down at the love of my life, whose laughter has suddenly died away as a delicate flush creeps up her neck. "Oh, sweetheart, there's only one thing I *need* to eat on this trip."

* * *

Thank you so much for reading! If you enjoyed this story, please take the time to leave a rating or review. It is such an enormous help for indie authors like myself, and I genuinely love hearing people's thoughts on my work!

    - Cleo

extended epilogue

WANT MORE ISSY **& Judah?** Check out this <u>bonus epilogue</u> with a spicy look into their new life together, set two weeks after Evie & Reuben's wedding.

also by cleo white

In the mood for more forbidden, age-gap, spicy goodness? Check out Cleo's other books!

Out of Sight

In Pieces

Age of Shade

You're It

Second Edition

Daddy Issues Series

Chilled and Thrilled

Kissed and Missed

Charmed and Alarmed

about the author

Cleo White's affinity for all things dramatic, and hopelessly romantic began the day she was born, which happened to be in the middle of a record-breaking snowstorm on Valentine's Day. Her love of literature came soon after, and she spent the better part of her childhood with both a book and a notebook full of unfinished stories in hand. Later in life, she found a love of writing spicy books with complicated characters and dysfunctional family drama. Cleo currently lives in Vermont with her husband and two daughters. When not writing, she can be found hiking, gardening, painting, and consuming excessive quantities of caffeine.

To stay up to date with upcoming releases and receive exclusive bonus content, subscribe to my newsletter at <u>www.authorcleowhite.com</u>